Empress of Wolves

Empress of Wolves

Evalyce – Worldshaper Book 3

J. Aislynn D' Merricksson

Published 2016 by Creativia

Book design by Creativia (www.creativia.org)

Cover art by http://www.thecovercollection.com/

Visit Port Jericho!

www.aislynndmerricksson.com

Visit our Facebook page!

www.facebook.com/Evalyce

*This book is dedicated those who are my life-blood
and strong, loving support:
To Brother Wildfire and Mercurius Greyeyes, my deepest
inspirations.
To Jonas Merricksson, twice lucky one, my callowayla.
To Beth Finley, who inspired me to open the door to De Sikkari.
To Michael Calabrase, Goshen, my soul-mate and nemesis.
To Chris and Brandi Gore, anamcara and truest of friends.*

To John and Sam Owens, my steady and strong support.

*To Anish and Tania, who helped make this possible!
To my family of heart and soul,
To my blood-family and
To my bond-family-
There are far too many of you to name here! I love you all the
same, each and every one.
In loving memory of Nina Clark
who taught me my own Dance
and fostered in me a love of learning.
May the One who is All And Nothing
forever guide your steps.
Nasmala!*

Contents

The Praetorian Guard

Argoth, 10000 ft. above the Aryth Ocean, Year of the Mythril Serpent, 2014 CE

It was the *Kujata* who greeted the travelers once more and it was the Admiral himself who flagged the ship. Kalla had no doubt the strike fighters, circling at a greater distance than usual, had warned the flagship of their approach. Who else might be traveling with wyvern, after all?

"This is Admiral Karlgraffsson, of the Imperial Flagship Kujata. *The borders to Argoth are currently closed. Please bring your ship into the* Kujata."

Kalla shook her head with a feeling of deja vu and wondered at the Admiral's formality.

"Acknowledged," she responded, replacing the radio as Aleister guided the ship into the same bay they had occupied before. He snugged it in place as the wyvern landed, hanging back by the hanger doors. Kasai joined them. The hawk was tense and watchful, clearly considering this enemy territory and Kalla couldn't say she blamed him. An aide scurried up. His worried gaze took in the extra people, focusing on Vander's robes.

"Greetings, Lady kyl'Solidor. Lord kyl'Solidor," he said with a bow. He led them to the same great-room that Ventaal had seen them in on their previous visit. Once more the Admiral waited within and, as before, waited until the aide was gone before losing the formalities.

"You've changed," Ventaal said as he hugged her. "What's with the new look?"

Kalla laughed. "That is a long story, Ventaal. A very, very long story. But tell me, what is going on? What news of Argoth?" she asked. The Admiral heaved a sigh.

"That, too, is a long story. Shall we trade then?" he asked. He eyed the rings she and Aleister wore with a sly grin, as if he suspected what they were. "And who are your companions?"

"Aahh, yes. Admiral Karlgraffsson, this is Vander kyl'Solidor and Magister Inaba Kasai.

"Vander, meet the master of the *Kujata*, Admiral Ventaal Karlgraffsson. Ventaal also happens to be an old friend."

"I am honored, Admiral," Vander said, inclining his head politely. Kasai echoed him, still tense and watchful.

"The pleasure is all mine," Ventaal said. "I welcome you both to my demesne, such as it is."

The Admiral invited them to sit at the great burnished oak table dominating the room, then called the aide back in and asked for refreshments to be brought. They passed the time until the aide returned in idle conversation. After he left, Kalla delved into her tale in earnest, telling Ventaal everything, beginning with her last trip to Argoth and ending with the group's stay in Dashmar. When she finished the Admiral ran a hand through his greying hair. Tired eyes the color of well-aged ale regarded her with an assessing look.

"That's an awful lot to take in all at once," he said after a time. "Hard to believe as well, though I can hardly deny that *something* has healed the land.

"Shards, Kalla! Waking Divinity and Empress of Dashmar? What have you gotten yourself into? But if you've truly done all of that, then maybe there is hope for us yet. Sykes does indeed seem under some sort of otherworldly influence. He is not acting himself. Hence the formality. Entry into Argoth is still severely limited. Glad I am that you approached from Zinlin. I don't think the other Admirals would have been as accommodating, especially our nearest neighbors. The Admiral of the *Barghast* has become increasing surly of late. Kosten would have turned you away, magi or not."

Ventaal went on to tell Kalla of all that had happened recently. Of Grosso's visits and the Emperor's increasing paranoia. Of Sykes' plans to attack Rang'moori. Kalla winced at that. They'd guessed right, but managed to get here before the Fleet had been officially mobilized.

"I will radio the *Phoenix*, telling them that the Dashmari ruler wishes to meet with Sykes. If we are lucky, Grosso will not yet know that his puppet has been deposed. You can get close enough to the Emperor to do something," Ventaal said.

"I thank you, Ventaal. Any help would be appreciated. That's a good idea, one I didn't think of. With Aleister's help, we can disguise ourselves. I just hope killing Sykes isn't necessary, but then, I have no need to challenge him as I did with Kartoff," Kalla replied. She turned to Vander.

"Think you can pull off being the Emperor of Dashmar?" she asked. Vander blinked.

"Me? You want *me* to do that?"

"Well, yes. You are Kartoff's son after all. I don't think I can quite get away with playing the part of a male."

"What about Kasai or Aleister?"

"Our job is to protect you and Kalla. It would look very strange, should things go wrong, for the Emperor to put himself in danger to save a mere soldier," Kasai said.

"Yes… I guess you're right… it's just… it will be strange, to try and pretend to be Kartoff."

Kalla put a reassuring hand on the War Mage's shoulder. "You'll do just fine. Don't worry." She looked to Ventaal. "Admiral?"

Ventaal punched the intercom button.

"*Yes, Admiral Karlgraffsson?*"

"Commander Kierksson, contact the *Phoenix*. Tell them the Dashmari ruler wishes to meet with Emperor Sykes, to discuss a mutually beneficial partnership. Ask if we may send them in with an escort from the *Kujata*."

"*Yes, Admiral,*" Kierksson replied.

"Now we wait. It may be some time before the *Phoenix* responds," the Admiral said. He favored Kalla with another assessing look. "*Liya,* hmm? Congratulations, Kalla. Melaric would be proud." He turned his gaze to Aleister.

"Of you, too, son. I knew I'd seen your ship before. It's good to know what happened to Melaric. I never thought he could have been so careless, storm or not. Take good care of both of them! Kalla and the *Stymphalian.*"

"Yessir, I intend to," Aleister replied, a bit sheepishly.

Ventaal laughed, a deep, genuine laugh, the first Kalla had heard from him during their visit.

"We should make our plans," Kalla said with a scowl. They were deep in discussion when the intercom crackled to life once more.

"*Admiral Karlgraffsson? The* Phoenix *has given permission for the Dashmari leader to pass the borders. The* Kujata *is to escort them in. Orders have been relayed to the* Barghast *and* Tengu *to widen their patrols.*"

Ventaal raised his eyebrows at this news. "Very well, Commander. Lay in a course for Argoth," he replied.

"*Yes, Admiral. Anything else?*"

"No, Commander, that will be all." Ventaal clicked the intercom off and looked to Kalla. "I guess you will be our guests until we arrive at Argoth."

Kalla and her companions spent the final distance to the great skycity with the Admiral, on the *Kujata's* bridge. Before they had left the great-room, Aleister had cloaked them in illusion, changing their clothes back to the uniforms of the Donnerkeil and once more altering his and Kasai's appearance to that of the Dashmari and Vander's to that of Kartoff's.

As they approached, Kalla could sense something different about the skycity. Things seemed ready for quiet and efficient action at a moment's notice. Activity along the Wall had increased and the guns tracked even the *Kujata* as she approached. Where the Healer had seen the *Barghast* during her last visit, the *Phoenix* now loomed, beautiful and terrifying at the same time. The Grand Flagship was three times the size of the largest flagship and held enough strike-fighters to be a city in and of itself. The *Phoenix* alone would be enough to deal with Rang'moori, never-mind the lesser flagships.

Ventaal escorted them to their ship. The hanger crew had changed, and word of a Dashmari presence on the ship had spread, so no mention of their change in appearance was made. The Admiral bid them farewell and wished them the best of luck. With a bow, Kasai made his way back to Thiassi, while the others boarded the *Stymphalian*. Kalla shared a final look with Ventaal before she disappeared into the shadowed depths of the ship and the doors slid shut behind her.

* * *

The Healer sighed as Aleister brought the ship down at a military paddock much closer to Imperia Argosia than their last stop had been. It would be but a short trip from here to the Imperial capital. Kalla was nervous. Though Aleister had disguised the group, there was little disguising the wyvern. She hoped no one would connect the red wyvern with the one that had accompanied the Argosian mage several months ago. Both wyvern coiled protectively around the strike-fighter after everyone was off.

They were greeted by an official procession, more impressive than the last. The Argosians all bowed deeply to the group, focusing on Vander. Clearly someone had told them what to expect of the Dashmari Emperor.

"Greetings and welcome to Argoth, Emperor Kartoff," the lead dignitary said. Vander's eyes narrowed dangerously. He gave a stiff nod back.

"I thank you. However, I would know how you knew my name?" His voice was ice. The dignitary faltered.

"From the Admiral, of course," he stammered in response.

"Interesting. I did not take the Admiral for one gifted in magick," Vander said.

"Magick, Your Grace?"

"I don't recall giving the good Admiral my name. He must, therefore, have magick to have been able to tell it to you. Such a shame that his talent was lost to the Kanlon," Vander replied in the same icy voice. The dignitary swallowed hard, confused and muddled by 'Kartoff's' reaction.

Kalla laughed inwardly, enjoying the trap Vander had sprung. Ventaal had never once mentioned the name Kartoff, so how indeed would the officials know.

Vander waved his hand in a negating gesture. "No matter. No matter at all. Please, do lead on. I look forward to meeting with Emperor Sykes."

The dignitary let out a slow breath, relieved at not having to explain how he had known the Dashmari ruler's name. More than any other nation, Grosso would want to hide his involvement with Argoth, a nation that could potentially be a threat to the Kanlon itself.

"Of course, Your Grace. Please, follow us. There are carriages waiting to take you to Imperia Argosia. The trip will take about an hour. Is there anything you wish before we leave?"

"I trust my ship will be in good hands here?" Kartoff' asked.

"The best, Your Grace. If I may ask, how is it that you came to be in possession of an Argosian ship?"

"I confiscated it from a pair of magi foolish enough to challenge me," he said. The officials blanched at his words, but said nothing.

"And my wyvern? Is there a place for them to hunt?"

"We... ahh... we can let them hunt in the woods near here," the dignitary said nervously.

"Very well. I would be most displeased if anything untoward were to befall them."

"No, Your Grace. They will be just fine here. You have my word. If you please?" The dignitary gestured towards the gates.

Kalla started to follow Vander, but the familiarity of an agitated voice pulled her around. Kasai must have told him she was distracted because the War Mage turned back to her, following her gaze to where Manny kyl'Malkador was wearily arguing with a military officer. Apparently the young Mage was not being allowed to leave the military compound and continue on in his quest for a magister. Argoth's condemned criminals were held in the Golden Court, the main prison, within Imperia Argosia. Vander dipped his head close to hers, speaking in a very soft voice.

"Invite him to come with us? He seems to be having problems," Vander murmured.

Kalla nodded. Since she was acting as Kartoff's aide, she was the one who walked over to Manny, Aleister keeping pace with her. She bowed to the Healer as she approached.

"Pardon my intrusion, Lord kyl'Malkador, but I wonder if I might trouble you for some of your time?" Kalla asked. Manny turned to her, a frustrated look on his face, unhappy at the interruption. His eyes widened slightly in puzzled recognition at the sound of her voice.

"K-"

"If it please you, my Lord, Emperor Kartoff would like to speak with you. We have been looking for one such as yourself. Perhaps you would care to join us?" she said, cutting him off before he could get her name out. Manny's eyes narrowed. He gave a slight nod, playing along with her.

"I would be honored," he said. She bowed again and beckoned him to follow. The Healer fell in step beside her, his body far vibrating with the desire to ask questions. Vander gave him a respectful nod as they approached.

"I am delighted to see that you accepted my invitation," he said. Manny returned the nod with a bow and Kalla chuckled inside. He was still young and sheltered enough to be intimidated by a ruler. Kalla wondered how long it had been since she'd felt that way. Her first experience with such a sovereign had been with the Khan Arkaddia when she had traveled with Hauss to heal the plague. She had acted the same way, much to both Hauss' and Nobunaga's amusement.

"I thank you, Emperor Kartoff. You are most generous," Manny said.

Vander's mouth turned up in a very slight smile before he turned back to the waiting dignitaries. They stood with crossed arms, deep frowns creasing their faces.

"I trust there will be no problem with my choice to have the mage accompany me?" he asked.

"No, Your Grace," the lead dignitary said in a slightly disgruntled tone that Vander chose not to acknowledge. Kalla wondered how long they had been stalling Manny. She sighed softly. They would have to teach him to throw his weight around. Magi had Pass Rights everywhere, just as the Harpers did. To refuse them was a grave offense to the Kanlon.

The 'Emperor' fell back in step with the officials, with Manny just behind him and the rest of them following behind. They were taken to a pair of carriages and, at Vander's insistence, his group was allowed to occupy one together. It was clear to Kalla that they wanted to separate Kartoff from his soldiers and from Manny, considering the two male Dashmari a greater threat than his female aide.

Kalla settled back with a sigh as the doors closed and a hand rapped against the side, signaling the driver to start moving. Manny opened his mouth, but she shook her head, putting a finger to her lips. His mouth thinned in a frown. The young mage ran a hand through his hair, massaging one temple with his thumb. Kalla held out her hand. Manny placed his into it and she forged a temporary link with him.

"*Lady Kalla?*"

"*Don't call me that. Just Kalla. You need to learn not to be intimidated by the trappings of power. You are magi, you are Lord kyl'Malkador, and you are above all of that,*" she said.

He huffed a sigh in her mind.

"*I know. It's hard though. But Kalla, why are you disguised as a Dashmari and why are you traveling with the Dashmari Emperor? And where are your magisters?*" he asked nervously.

"*Long story and my magisters still travel with me. You will learn soon enough. You looked as though you could use some help.*"

"*Yes. I've been here for two weeks. I keep getting put off. I was almost ready to give up and leave Argoth altogether. I'm glad I didn't!*" he said with a laugh.

Kalla gave him a grin and gently drew her hand free, breaking the link. Kartoff drew him into conversation, while she sat, watchful and patient, with the two Magisters.

Imperia Argosia, Argoth, Year of the Mythril Serpent, 2014 CE

The Imperial capital was a sprawling, busy city. Wide avenues lined with huge fir trees were laid out in a neat grid-work. Shops, temples, homes, warehouses and all manner of other buildings lined the broad streets.

They stopped at a military checkpoint close to the Evergreen Palace, one flanking the massive Golden Court and well within the prison's palisade. The prison itself was crafted from burnt orange granite. Narrow, barred windows were sparsely placed along the two story building. The columns before the Golden Court were carved in the likeness of autumn trees, mostly bare of leaves, and images of King Holly, the Argosian deity of autumn and winter, those seasons of death's slumber.

As they climbed out of the carriages a group exited the prison- six of the Praetorian Guard escorting a bound prisoner to the Court's execution grounds.

Kalla's eyes narrowed as she looked over the prisoner. His gait was proud, his head held high. The man wore the tattered, disheveled remains of a Guard uniform.

The uniforms consisted of a dark green tunic, black breeches, and black boots. A chain-mail vest of snakeskin was worn over the tunic. This was no ordinary snakeskin. Crafted from the skins of armour snakes, it was a very fine, lightweight, and flexible. A dark iridescent grey in color, snakeskin armour was strong enough to stop most weapons. A black surcoat open to the front, with the Trinity Claw of House Sykes embroidered on the back, was worn over the mail. Each Guard had a sword belted at the waist, and a holster slung across their backs held the trade-mark weaponry of the elite Praetorian Guard- a short-barreled rifle.

The Praetorian Guard were the best of the Argosian military, and the personal Guard of the Emperor himself. Kalla wondered what one of them could possibly have done that warranted his execution. She also knew that Manny could do no worse for a magister, if the man would accept. She reached out and touched his hand, reforging the link between them, even as the Guards shoved the prisoner to his knees against the inner wall of the palisade that surrounded the Golden Court.

"*Time to learn to throw your weight around, Lord kyl'Malkador. That man is one of the Praetorian Guard. You could find no better choice, save among the Harriers of Arkaddia. And trust me when*

I say that might make the Khan a bit upset at the moment," she said with a dry laugh.

Manny swallowed hard, but took a decisive step forward and when he spoke, it was in a strong voice.

"Stop!" The young Healer's voice rang across the courtyard. The Guards froze and looked over at Kalla's group. Their guides spun around, agitated. Before they could say anything, Manny was already striding from the path, crossing the courtyard to where the prisoner knelt. The man looked up as the mage approached, his face tired, but fiercely proud. The captive Guard was an older gentleman, his black hair turning a gunmetal grey.

The Guards had backed off, scowling at the mage. Kalla was too far way to hear what Manny said to the prisoner, but they exchanged a lengthy conversation that earned several angry looks from the Guards. Finally the man nodded wearily, bowing his head as Manny crouched down before him.

Manny made a small gesture and the man's shackles fell away. The prisoner shrugged his shoulders and rubbed his wrists, but remained kneeling where he was. He didn't flinch as Manny reached out and placed hands to his face. A few moments passed, then Manny rose to his feet, offering a hand to help the man up.

The dignitaries frowns deepened as Manny spoke with the Guards, then disappeared into the Golden Court with them, followed by his new magister. Unmoved by assurances that Manny would be brought to the Evergreen Palace, Kartoff insisted that they be allowed to follow him. Their guides finally gave up and escorted the Dashmari into the prison. The Guards inside took them to a room where Manny waited while his magister was cleaned up and properly clothed.

"I see you found what you were looking for, Lord kyl'Malkador," Kartoff said.

"Yes, my Lord. I thank you. If not for your intervention, I wouldn't have gotten this far," Manny replied. "Lukas Aricsson, former Praetor, accused of treason and attempted assassination.

He tells an interesting story though. Says he wasn't trying to kill Emperor Sykes, but rather Grosso, who is apparently interfering with the Imperial Court."

As if speaking of him had summoned him, voices outside the door heralded the arrival of Lukas, looking much more presentable than he had outside.

The former Praetor was dressed in a Guard uniform sans the surcoat. A shortsword hung at his side, balanced by a bullet pouch on the other side. One of the rifles rested against his back. Lukas bowed to them, his movements deadly grace.

"Lord kyl'Malkador, Your Grace," Lukas said. He bowed deeply, fist to chest in the Argosian way. Eyes the color of evergreen pines assessed the four Dashmari. His voice held the easy drawl that characterized most Argosian speech. Quick as foxes in their thinking, yet most of Argoth's citizenry drawled their words in a lazy tone, hiding just how cunning and clever they could be. Kalla hid a smile. It had been a long time since she had heard an Argosian with such a pronounced accent as Lukas'. If she had to wager a guess, she'd say he was from northern Argoth.

"Well met, Magister Aricsson," Vander replied. The man winced, a mere tightening of the skin around his eyes, but Kalla caught it. He was still trying to figure out how he felt about his new situation.

"Sir Lukas, you will be traveling to the Evergreen Palace with us. Is that going to be a problem for you?" Vander asked. Lukas winced again, but shook his head.

"No, Your Grace. Emperor Sykes will likely not be pleased, but I have been fairly claimed as a magister of the Kanlon. I am grateful for a chance to maybe put things right.

"I will warn you though, Your Grace, that there is another mage here already, interfering where the magi are forbidden to interfere," Lukas said, voice tight with anger and tension.

"Yes, Lord kyl'Malkador has shared that with me. Perhaps we will be able to do something about that, in the end," Vander replied.

"I would be in your debt," Lukas said with a bow. Now that Lukas was done, the Guards lead them back to the waiting dignitaries.

"I think we are finished here. Please, do lead on," Vander said. They scowled at him, giving Lukas an even more unfriendly look. Kalla guessed that news of Manny's new magister would precede them to the Palace and Sykes would be fully aware of the situation long before they arrived. She hadn't missed the Guard that had spoken to their guides, then took off at a trot.

As they filed out of the prison and started up the wide avenue that would lead them to the Evergreen Palace, the three magisters spread out to surround Kalla, 'Kartoff' and Manny. Lukas easily and instinctively worked with the two soldiers, not realizing that they were magisters as well. Kasai took the point of the protective triangle, Aleister the left and Lukas the right. A phalanx of the Guard surrounded them, ostensibly as an escort.

The group rounded the corner, turning onto another broad avenue. The Evergreen Palace dominated the street's end. Carved from a dark green granite, the Palace rose in elegant tree towers, Trinity Crown banners snapping and fluttering from the tops.

Columns before the Imperial Palace were carved with images of green thriving trees and depictions of King Oak, the deity of spring and summer, the seasons of life's exultation. Two rows of Royal Pines lined the sides of the avenue, while a single row of giant Regal Oaks ran up the center. The street was broad enough for columns of soldiers to pass up or down either side. Nearby a small river burbled, an offshoot of the great Algassey River.

More of the Praetorian Guard stood at attention before the Palace. They bowed as the procession approached them. A tall man stepped forward. He was dressed in pants and tunic of a hunter green. The collar and sleeves were embroidered with gold thread in a tiny leaf pattern. Over this he wore a black tabard with the Trinity Claw on the back.

"Greetings, Emperor Kartoff, and welcome to Imperia Argosia. My name is Owyn Jacobsson, Castellan of the Evergreen. If you will please follow me, the Emperor is waiting to meet you." Owyn paused. His eyes narrowed as his gaze settled on Lukas.

"I must, however, ask that the mage and his... magister remain here. The servants will take them to comfortable quarters."

"We would be delighted to accompany you. All of us, that is, for I am afraid I must insist that the mage stay with us." Vander moved so that both Manny and Lukas were behind him. "I have invited him to join my party, thus making him my responsibility. Until we should choose to part ways, he is of my pack and entitled to the same such courtesy as the rest. Are you implying that I should also let my soldiers be taken to 'comfortable quarters' as well," he asked in a flat voice.

"No, Your Grace. The soldiers can accompany you. They are Dashmari. The Mage is not..."

"Who are you, to tell me whom I can consider pack, Castellan? I value his company and he is mine to protect. If this is how I am to be treated, I think I may as well leave now and curse the fact that I have traveled so far," 'Kartoff' growled.

Owyn's jaws tightened and Kalla could almost hear his teeth grinding. She wanted to laugh, for Vander's performance was wonderful. He was a good actor, she had to give him that. Through their bond, she felt Aleister's amusement as well. The Castellan came to a sudden decision and nodded abruptly towards Vander.

"Very well. He may stay with you," Owyn said reluctantly. Vander gave him a grin, baring long canine teeth. The Dashmari sported prominent fangs, another legacy from the frost wolves. The Castellan paled slightly, instinctively understanding the implied threat in Vander's gesture. It was a look that, while neutral or mirthful for most people, for a Dashmari, said 'I'll be more than happy to rip your throat out, if you keep annoying me.'

"Thank you, Castellan," Vander said in a polite voice. Through the entire exchange, Manny had stayed silent, apparently trusting Kalla's judgment that he would be safe in the Dashmari 'Emperor's' hands.

Accompanied by their Guard escort, the followed Owyn to the Emperor's throne room. As they approached, another of the Guard, posted outside the throne room, rapped on the massive golden tree-wrought doors with a heavy, metal-tipped staff. An answering rap came from the other side, then the doors swung inward, pulled open by more of the Praetorian Guard within.

Lord of Leaves

Kalla's eyes were immediately drawn to the Evergreen Throne, crafted from a living Royal Pine that rose to the very top of the vaulted ceiling. A skylight above the throne let in light, and several times a day servants watered the stately tree. Upon this throne sat Elim Sykes, Lord of Leaves and Emperor of the Argosian Empire. Sykes wore an outfit similar to the Castellan, but of a much richer cut and without the tabard. A golden crown, woven in the shape of entwined leaves rested upon his head. Winks of green fire drew her attention to two rings on his hands, emeralds set in gold. One was the Imperial signet ring, the other a beautifully crafted oak leaf.

Before the throne, flanking it to either side, stood the current Praetor, and a woman in the uniform of the Argosian Fleet. Behind the woman stood a man who regarded them with lazy indifference.

The Praetor looked much like the Guards, the only difference in uniform being that his surcoat was edged in gold. He wore an oak leaf ring like Sykes', carved from carnelian, rather than emerald, and a Trinity Claw engraved in amethyst, the color of the Guard's rings. He was younger than Lukas, his hair still jet black. Bittersweet brown eyes regarded them with an impassivity that was frightening from one so young.

As they drew closer, Kalla's eyes widened slightly as she got a better look at the woman to Sykes' left. She wore the same ash-grey uniform that Ventaal did, but the braiding at her sleeve cuffs was different. The uniforms bore the Trinity Claw upon the right shoulder and the Flagship emblem upon the left. Ventaal's was a stylized silver elephant with an orb curled in its trunk. This lady had a golden bird clutching branches in its claws and was none other than the Fleet Admiral herself, the captain of the Grand Flagship *Phoenix*. Like all in the Fleet, she wore a ruby Trinity Claw ring. The Fleet Admiral caught Kalla's gaze and inclined her head politely.

The man behind the Admiral wore steel-grey robes with the same golden bird on one shoulder. An eagle and snake emblem graced the other. This man, then, was the *sa'mir* or Chief Technomancer, of the *Phoenix*. The Technomancers were a part of the Fleet. Magick users with a more technological bent, they served Mercurius, the Argosian deity of magick and the martial world.

Kalla was honestly surprised that the children of the Clockwork God would suffer another magick-user to interfere with their Emperor, and she prayed a quick prayer that Grosso had not managed to corrupt the *se'tov*, the leaders of the Technomancers. A flagship's Chief Technomancer could overrule the Admiral and take control of the ship, quite literally, if the *sa'mir* happened to be an Old One or had an *al'raj* with them. It would do them no good to free Sykes, if the Technomancers went rogue.

The Kanlon held an uneasy peace with Argoth's magick-users, but if it came to a true fight there was no doubt in the Healer's mind as to which group would win...

Sykes rose as they approached, stepping down to stand between Praetor and Admiral. His eyes narrowed slightly as he took in Manny and Lukas, but he chose to ignore the presence of his former Praetor.

"Greetings, Emperor Kartoff, and welcome to Argoth. I trust your visit thus far has been satisfactory. Night draws near. Will you, perhaps, join us for dinner and we can discuss business matters upon the 'morrow? No doubt you are tired after your travels." Sykes asked.

"Greetings, Emperor Sykes. Well met. We would be honored to join you. As you say, business can wait," Kartoff replied. He stepped back and gestured to Manny. "May I introduce Manny kyl'Malkador?"

"Greetings, Lord kyl'Malkador. Welcome to Argoth," Sykes nodded to the young Mage.

"Lord kyl'Malkador is my guest for the time being. You will have no objection to him joining us, né?"

The slightest of grimaces flitted across the Argosian Emperor's face, gone as quickly as it had come.

"Of course not, Emperor Kartoff," he replied.

Kalla tensed as a whisper of power curled through the throne room. She shivered as the power caressed her, assessing her, then discounting her. The Healer recognized the feel of it. Solidor's former Tem' was somewhere within the Evergreen Palace, though not close enough to locate.

Before her, Kalla saw an almost unnoticeable tremor run through Vander as the power touched him. Beside her Manny shivered, glancing around nervously. The Technomancer's eyes narrowed and he scowled faintly. Clearly he could sense the mental intrusion and disliked it. Grosso's power receded, apparently satisfied enough that they were what they seemed to be. No doubt he would seek out Kartoff later and then what would be, would be. Sykes and those with him noticed nothing different, or if they did, they didn't betray it. Kalla sighed with relief as the rogue mage's power faded away. The Fox's own brand of magick had held firm against the inquisitive intrusion.

"If you will please follow us then." Sykes gestured towards a door past the throne. He turned to follow his Praetor, the Fleet Admiral and her *sa'mir* falling behind him. They ended up in a small dining room just perfect for a group their size. Servants seated the group, Dashmari soldiers included, and in due order came bustling back with a dinner of potato dumplings, baked partridge and a mix of sautéed squashes.

Apparently Grosso had at least told them to allow the Dashmari soldiers to dine with their Emperor. It would have been seen as a weakness for them to actually stand guard over Kartoff, undermining his authority as an alpha able to take care of himself. They were guards, yes, but they were also his pack. As lesser wolves they would not eat *until* Kartoff had, but they would eat *with* him. She also realized that the Argosians had subconsciously picked her as his second, his Dashtela. Kalla fought the urge to laugh hysterically at that notion and earned a covert worried look from Aleister.

Dinner passed with little incident. Kalla, and the magisters, paid a watchful attention to the goings-on, though little mind was paid to them. She learned that the Fleet Admiral's name was Tabitha Ryansdottr, her *sa'mir* was Lefellus, and the new Praetor was James Everettsson.

Nor did Sir James care for Lukas' presence, but the newly raised magister steadfastly ignored the younger man's veiled hostility. Sykes, for his part, chose to ignore the former Praetor, but the Healer sensed his tension. From Lukas, she sensed a great deal of bitterness. Sykes was a man he had once called friend, and his misconstrued actions to protect Sykes had shattered the bond between them. What Kalla would like to ask Lukas was why a truth-read on him not been done by one of the Technomancers.

The tense meal finished and Sykes himself led the Dashmari to the quarters that had been arranged for them. It was a large room from which most of the furnishings had been hastily re-

moved. Piles of blankets and pillows had been left for the Dashmari to make their own pallets, and the Healer realized with
a start how very similar the Dashmari were to the Arkaddians in that respect, preferring nests on the ground to beds with
mattresses. Kartoff gestured for Manny to precede him into the
room, preventing any attempt to separate the mage from his
group. Sir James started to protest, but Sykes stopped him with
an upraised hand. The Praetor subsided into angry fuming, but
said nothing.

"Emperor Kartoff, could I perhaps speak with you privately
for a moment?" he asked. Kartoff followed him down the hall
a short bit, out of earshot, but still within sight of the Praetor
and the Dashmari soldiers. The two briefly conversed, and the
groups parted ways.

Vander gave a sigh of relief and leaned against the closed
door. "Emperor Sykes would like me to know I am harboring
a traitor. He understands that Lukas is now magister, but thinks
I would do well to watch my back."

Lukas snorted. "I have no intention of harming either you or
Emperor Sykes, Your Grace," he drawled. "The other mage, how-
ever, he's a different story, he is. If I get another chance at him,
I intend to take it."

"I wouldn't advise that, Sir Lukas," Kalla said quietly. "If something should happen to you, your mage will share it with you.
And if you should die, he would feel it very clearly. Rest assured,
things will be taken care of, one way or another."

"K-" Manny once more tried to say the Healer's name, but
she again cut him off.

"Peace, Lord kyl'Malkador. All things in due time." Her ears
flicked, twitching nervously. Beside her, both Aleister and Kasai
let out low growls, their own ears pricking forward.

"We are going to have company. Don't be alarmed, and don't
do anything rash. Above all, don't allow yourselves to be baited,"
Vander said.

Even as he spoke there was a soft crack of power and Grosso stood before them, looking slightly annoyed. Kalla had to stifle a gasp at seeing the Artisan once more. The wounds they had inflicted on him in Arkaddia were healed now, albeit very inexpertly. Rough, uneven scarring covered parts of the right side of his face and what she could see of his right arm. His hand no longer seemed to function properly and, when he moved, it was with noticeable difficulty. Pale blue eyes regarded them with a flat emotionlessness.

"What are you doing here?" Grosso hissed. "And why does another mage travel with you?" The Artisan ignored the others, though the dislike from both Lukas and Kasai was near stifling to Kalla's sensitive senses. She guessed it was just as bad for Vander, but he didn't drop his act, even in the least way.

"I figured it wouldn't hurt to seek out alliances among those you've been working with. As for the other mage, he is a Healer. I have need of one." Kartoff growled out the last in angry tones and Grosso flinched, just a bit.

"My... apologies, Emperor. It will not happen again."

"I daresay not," Kartoff replied in a curt tone. Grosso's eyes narrowed dangerously.

"They say you came in on your own ship, Your Grace. You've been busy."

"Yes, I took it from a pair of meddling magi who sought to challenge me."

"Challenge you?"

"Yes, indeed. A young Dashmari mage, Kalla her name was. The one you spoke of, with my son in tow. She challenged me for rulership and chose to play by the rules. No offensive magick. What the pup hoped to accomplish, I can't say. I won the ship and decided to make use of it, so here I am."

"And what of Vander?"

"The elemental took care of him when the pup lost the battle," Kartoff said.

The Artisan snorted. "A fitting end. Finish your business here quickly, Emperor, so that I may finish mine."

"Oh, don't worry. Things will be over before you know it."

"Just so. See that it is." Grosso gave Kartoff a suspicious look, cast another towards Lukas, and disappeared.

Manny turned to Kalla after the Artisan had departed.

"With all due respect, Lady, *what* is going on here?" he asked.

Kalla shook her head and held out a hand to both Manny and Lukas. The Malkadoran Healer took it readily enough, but Lukas gave her a distrustful look, only reluctantly taking the proffered hand.

"*Emperor Kartoff was Grosso's puppet. We deposed the Dashmari ruler. The man you see before you is Vander. The other two would be Aleister and Vander's new magister, Inaba Kasai, formerly Master Harrier of Arkaddia.*"

Manny and Lukas glanced over to where the two magisters lounged against the wall. Aleister gave them a sly grin, Kasai a curt nod.

"Master Harrier? *But I thought Vander was your magister now?*" Manny asked.

"*I think it will be easier to show you what we've been going through, than to tell it,*" Kalla said wearily.

Manny nodded and she opened memory links between her and the younger Healer and his magister. She took them through her memories of entering Xibalba and meeting Araun. Vander's transformation and his new skills. Her realization of who and what she and Aleister really were. Of healing Arkaddia and freeing the Khan. Grosso's involvement with Nobunaga and his subsequent flight. Aleister's injury, the breaking of her bond with Vander and his acquisition of a new magister. Their deaths and resurrection. The visit to the Hounds, her summoning of Araun and the truth behind the Lord of Living Nightmare. The *li'saal* ceremony.

She guided them through their third meeting with Araun, their departure from Arkaddia and arrival at Dashmar. Aleister's growing command of his innate fox-magick. The challenge and deposing of Emperor Kartoff. Their stay in Dashmar and the return to Argoth to free Sykes from Grosso's influence.

When she was finished, she stopped the flow of memory. Manny met her gaze with a dazed look, and he started to jerk his hand away with a mixture of awe and fear. The Solidoran Healer sighed. She was getting tired of this reaction and she gripped his hand tighter, not letting him pull away.

"*I am still Kalla. Here and now, I am Kalla.*"

"*Great Fen'raal, you are* not *just Kalla,*" Manny breathed. "*And* liya, *Lady Kalla? Not that I am not happy for you, but isn't that what's not supposed to happen?*"

"*Yes, well, I think the Prince can take care of himself.*"

"*You've been busy, Lady Kalla. What is your plan now? And why did you bring me along anyway?*"

"*You looked as if you could use some help. And in the end, you found what you were looking for, did you not, and saved an innocent man's life too. You know as well as I that Lukas is telling the truth,*" she replied. "*As for our plan, that's still unfolding.*"

"*Thank you for helping me, helping both of us. I guess we should leave soon, to go back to the Kanlon.*"

"*May we stay with you until this is resolved? Until you free Sykes?*" Manny asked.

"*I have no objections to your staying. If you wish, perhaps Vander would even begin working with you.*" Kalla laughed as she caught the younger Healer's dubious look. "*Lesson number one, don't be fooled by first appearances. The War Mage is actually a very good teacher, and a much different person than before. He is what he was meant to be, now.*"

It was Manny's turn to nod. "*Very well, Lady Kalla. Thank you for letting us stay. I will ask Vander for help.*"

His words were interrupted by a soft whistling from Aleister. A moment's pause, then Vander looked at Manny with an assessing look.

"I would be glad to help," he said.

Manny's eyes widened. "I, but…" he sputtered. Kalla squeezed his hand gently in warning.

"*I thought you could no longer speak with him!*"

"*Aleister told him. Or rather, Aleister told his brother, who told him. The Harriers have their own language and, as you saw, Aleister spent a fair bit of time during our stay in Arkaddia with the hawks. The Fox is quick and clever as his name. He learns fast.*"

"*For the time being, though, continue to act as if Vander and I are nothing more than Dashmari. Grosso could be listening. So far, Aleister's fox-magick has kept us concealed. I don't want to break that until the proper time,*" Kalla said.

"*Yes, Lady Kalla,*" Manny said in a subdued voice.

"*As you wish, milady,*" Lukas said. "*Thank you, both for letting us stay and for attempting to set things straight. I do so hope that you can take care of the rogue mage while you are at it.*"

"*We certainly intend to try,*" she replied. "*Sir Lukas, I have a question for you. Why was no truth-read done on you?*"

"*Well, milady, that mage, he convinced Sykes not to. Said everyone in the throne room had seen my actions. That included Master Lefellus and I guess the* sa'mir *agreed with the Emperor,*" Lukas replied. His gaze dropped, and his shoulders sagged. Kalla squeezed his hand, acknowledging his sadness, offering what comfort he could. Lukas looked up, giving her a tired smile.

The Healer gently tugged her hands free, working to stifle a yawn. "I suggest we make our beds now and get some rest. Tomorrow will no doubt prove to be a long day."

Following Kalla's lead, the group made nests out of the blankets and pillows that had been provided. Between Kasai and Aleister, the magisters arranged to keep a surreptitious guard, with the hawk taking first watch. With a regretful sigh, Aleister made his pallet far from Kalla, for in their new roles they were not *liya*. Lukas they encouraged to sleep. The man kept up a tough front, but his sojourn in the Golden Palace had not been kind.

The Healer didn't stop Manny from setting shields around the room though. They were not as strong as the War Mage's would have been, nor even Kalla's, but she didn't want to rouse any suspicion. Grosso would expect that he would shield the room, but the Artisan would know that the young Healer wasn't skilled enough in a Defensor's craft to create very strong shields, merely the basics all magi knew.

Evergreen Palace, Imperia Argosia, Argoth, Year of the Mythril Serpent, 2014 CE

Kalla rose bright and early, in the grey of pre-dawn, the time between times. The mage yawned and stretched, then threaded her way through her sleeping companions and out onto the balcony of their room. She stood for a time, staring out into the foggy morn as the sun slowly rose, sending streaks of rose and pink through the greyness.

"*Good morning, milady.*" Aleister's voice cut through her musings as he came out on the balcony to stand beside her, favoring her with a warm smile. "*Do you have any idea yet what Grosso might be using to control Sykes?*"

Kalla nodded.

"*I am fairly certain it is the second ring he wears. The one with the more elaborate Trinity Claw graven into it is the Imperial signet. The other though, seems to be a personal choice. Did you notice, the stone was cut like an oak leaf? Something of a spiritual significance to an Argosian, like the Spiral is to the Arkaddians and, unlike Kartoff's rings, it holds no obvious magick. But then, neither did the spiral pendant. Sykes is tinged with the same corruption as Nobunaga was. I fear the same will befall him, should*" *we destroy it. One or all three of us magi should be near him when we do destroy it.*"

Kalla turned and began pacing back and forth along the balcony, hands clasped behind her.

"*We have a bigger problem, though. Sir James is tainted as well and the corruption more firmly rooted. He, too, wears an oak leaf ring, though I haven't seen any others wearing one. The Fleet Admiral, thank the gods, is not tainted. The only thing worse would be if the Technomancer leadership has been corrupted. It seems unlikely though, if Grosso is sniffing around.*" Kalla said with a heavy sigh.

A slight noise behind the pair heralded the arrival of Vander and Kasai, the former yawning hugely. Kalla snorted at the 'Emperor's' undignified demeanour and held her hand out to him, establishing a link between them. She filled the pair in on what she and Aleister had been discussing.

"*I agree,*" Vander said. "*But stealing the rings as we did the pendant isn't an option. Moreover, I don't see how we can destroy both at the same time. As soon as there is any interference with Sykes, we will be attacked and we will need to react appropriately. I think the best bet would be to focus on the Emperor first and foremost. Trust me, Lady Kalla, I can craft the necessary shields to protect both you and Sykes. But as soon as we start using such magick, Grosso is sure to come running.*"

"*We will have to take our chances. I will see if I can draw the Emperor into conversation later and bring the ring up. If I can get him to slip it from his finger all the better. With Vander's shields, I can concentrate on destroying the ring, then the rest of you can cover me as I heal Sykes. Keep the Guard at bay. They will not be as trusting as the Harriers,*" Kalla said. "*We will also need to be prepared to deal with* sa'mir *Lefellus. The Technomancers use a different brand of magick than we do. Should he be present, we'll have an even larger problem to deal with.*"

A knock to the door interrupted their conversation. It was Owyn, come to invite them to join Sykes for their morning meal. They were taken to the same room they had dined in the night before, with the same assembly collected.

Two men had joined Emperor Sykes, both dressed in the formal clerical robes of the Argosian priesthood. They wore simple robes, one in shades of green and the other in shades of orange, belted with brown, tasseled cords. The men had precious little adornment. Wooden pendants carved into the likeness of oak and holly leaves hung about their necks and plain bands of malachite and carnelian were worn around the middle finger of the left hand. These were the High Clerics of Argoth, the Voice of King Holly and King Oak in the realm of men.

Sykes introduced them as Cleric Jonas Morgansson and Cleric Zacharias Eddasson. Jonas, the priest in orange, was the head of the Order of Holly. He was an older gentleman, closer in age to Sykes and Lukas. Stocky and muscular, he had a bulldog face. White salted his black hair and neatly trimmed beard.

Zacharias was younger, near to Manny's age. He was young to be head of the Order of Oak, Kalla reflected. Zacharias was taller than Jonas, with an unruly mane of black hair. A neat goatee was the only facial hair he sported. Dark brown eyes regarded the Dashmari with frank curiosity.

After breakfast was done and the table cleared and cleaned, the small dining room became a conference room.

"Well, Emperor Kartoff, why don't you tell me why you're here," Sykes asked bluntly. Kartoff regarded the Argosian Emperor a long moment, before speaking.

"I seek an alliance, Emperor Sykes. Dashmar has only recently become a truly unified country. We would benefit from creating alliances with other nations. My people have historically been a very reclusive one. I seek to change that. Already, border packs harbour Argosian mining enclaves"

"Why Argoth? Why not the Crannogmarch, Kymru or Rang'moori? Arkaddia even. They are all much closer."

"With all due respect, I believe you know the answer to that, Emperor," Kartoff said. Sykes gave a wry laugh.

"Indeed. And what is your proposal? What do you seek from us and what does Dashmar have to offer in trade?" he asked. Kartoff smiled grimly. He liked Sykes' blunt manner. He sincerely hoped nothing untoward would happen to the Lord of Leaves when they freed him.

"Dashmar is rich in metals and gems, as well as a great many other natural resources, including deposits of various mage metals, as you know. That is what I offer. What I seek…"

The two monarchs spent the morning in negotiation. Things progressed favorably and they talked late into the afternoon, taking only two short breaks. Sykes finally called things to an end, saying they would resume things after lunch. He had the servants lead them to an outdoor courtyard for a meal of water fowl over rice, mixed squashes, and ale.

Several of the Praetorian Guard were unobtrusively stationed around the courtyard's perimeter. The day was fairly mild and Kalla relished the chance to be outdoors. Here, too, it might be easier for her to speak to Sykes.

Her chance came sooner than she expected. After the group finished their meal they took their ease in the courtyard, relaxing a bit before retiring back to the conference room. Kalla approached Sykes alone after surreptitiously telling Vander to be ready to shield her at her signal. The War Mage idly paced the perimeter of the courtyard, seeming lost in conversation with the Fleet Admiral and her *sa'mir*. Kasai and Aleister trailed behind him, though the Fox was keeping a close eye on her.

"Pardon me, Your Grace, but I couldn't help noticing your ring. It is an unusual piece of craftsmanship. It is an Ishkaran emerald is it not, Clovis cut?" she asked. Sykes gave her an appraising look. Nearby, Sir James narrowed his eyes at her.

"Why yes, it is. You have a good eye," he replied.

"Few can perfect the Clovis cut. An Artisan of great talent must have created that piece. A rare find, even for an Emperor. Could I...?" Kalla paused, lowering her gaze. She was aware that Vander had completed his circuit of the courtyard and stopped behind her, still in conversation with the Admiral.

"Yes? Can you...?" Sykes prompted. She shook her head.

"Forgive me, Your Grace. It would be inappropriate of me to ask."

"Ask," he said gently.

"I merely wished to know if I might have a closer look."

"But of course. That is an easy enough request," he replied, slipping the ring off his finger and holding it out to her. She reached out shyly to take it from him.

"Thank you for your indulgence, Your Grace," she said as he carefully placed the ring in her hand. As soon as he had withdrawn his fingers, Kalla gestured with her free hand. In an instant, she felt the layered shields wrap around her. From Sykes expression he, too, felt the shields forming around his own person. Kalla held the ring up, clutched in her fist and ignited it with magefire. Sykes dropped to the ground with a stunned look as the magefire consumed the ring and its attendant corruption. Sir James drew his rifle, aiming for her.

At the same time, Vander activated the warding he had laid, but it was seconds too late. Two deafening shots rang through the courtyard, one from Sir James and a second from another of the Guard just before the warding closed. The Praetor's shot hit her first, destroying the carefully crafted shields. The second shot tore into her body, throwing her to the ground, and saving her from Lefellus' retaliation. A stone column across the courtyard shattered, spraying shards everywhere. Another shot rang out mere seconds later, hitting Sir James full in the chest. The Praetor crumpled to the ground, gave a feeble jerk and moved no more.

"NO! Milady!"

Kalla heard the Fox, but his voice seemed far away. All around her were shocked gasps and when she caught a glimpse of Vander as he strode towards her he was no longer disguised as Kartoff. She struggled to make her magick work, to begin mending the wound she'd received. It was bad, she could tell. Aleister stumbled to her side, sinking to the ground. If he was this disoriented, a cold part of Kalla's mind rationalized, then she must be dying. He gripped her hand, tears slipping down his cheeks.

Vander and Manny knelt between the two fallen, the mage and the Emperor. Vander did a quick assessment of Kalla's condition, frowning at what he found. He immediately began working on her.

"Manny, have you dealt in soul healing?" he asked, not looking up.

"Yes, Lord kyl'Solidor."

"Good. You work with Sykes then. We must save the Emperor at all costs. The destruction of the ring purged the corruption in his spirit. However, it had its own price," Vander replied.

Manny nodded and turned to work with Sykes, but a gruff voice pulled him away. He looked up to find the Technomancer towering above them. Lefellus knelt between Kalla and Sykes.

"I don't know what the pair of you are playing at," he snapped, "but a third wouldn't be amiss. You save him, or I'll execute you myself."

Vander met the Technomancer's fierce gaze, then nodded slightly. "Fair enough."

Lefellus snorted, lowering his hands and placing a palm on both patients' faces. Thin tendrils of metal seeped from the backs of his hands, spiderwebbing out and burrowing under flesh as roots to soil. Manny gasped and jerked away.

"Do your job, boy. I'll keep them stable."

The young Healer nodded shakily and warily settled back to his work with a final, frightened glance at the steel-faced Technomancer.

Kasai and Lukas stood a guard over the group, ringed in by the Praetorian Guard. Kasai had scooped up Sir James' rifle and held it as if he knew how to use it. Both magisters kept their rifles low, but remained wary. It had been Lukas who had kept the Harrier from lashing out in a futile attack on Lefellus when the Technomancer approached. The Argosian knew full well that, should Lefellus attack again, there wasn't much they could do.

Vander whispered softly to Kalla, trying to focus her attention, to keep her alert, as he healed the damage wrought by the rifle shot. He was still at a loss as to how a mere bullet could collapse his shields.

"Forgive me, Lady Kalla," Vander said as he gently cut away her clothing to better see the damage. He established microwards, as he had with Aleister, routing the blood back to its proper places. Vander found himself thankful for the Technomancer's assistance. The man had already strengthened the feeble stabilizers Kalla had managed to craft around her heart, the most damaged organ, and he was doing the job of keeping that heart beating and the lungs breathing. He was keeping both patients stabilized, Vander realized.

A sharp crack of power interrupted Vander. The War Mage jerked his head back up, a deep growl thrumming in his throat, and found Grosso standing next to Sir James' body. The Artisan's pale eyes were lit with an uncharacteristic rage.

Lukas and Kasai responded to the mage's appearance with lightning reflexes, bringing Guard rifles to bear on him. Kasai had claimed Sir James' rifle, and proved he was as adept with firearms as he was with other weapons. A shot rang out, colliding full on with Grosso, destroying his shields. A second shot barely missed him as he stooped and grabbed a handful of the Praetor's clothing and disappeared.

Kasai snarled something in Arkaddian that made Aleister look up with bleary eyes. The fallen magister was looking better and growing stronger as Vander worked to heal Kalla. Vander spared a brief moment to wonder why the Artisan would want to take the Praetor's body with him, but cast those thoughts aside and resumed his work. Grosso was gone now, of that he was certain, and Al'dhumarna's corruption gone with him.

Some time later, the War Mage sighed and sat back. He rubbed gritty eyes, thankful to finally be finished with his work. At some point, Manny had replaced Lefellus. The young Healer had brought Sykes back from the edge of the abyss. The Technomancer had given his Emperor a full looking over and, at the Fleet Admiral's instruction, several of the Guard had gently carried Sykes to his quarters, there to be tended to by the two Clerics. Master Lefellus had withdrawn his assistance, but had remained with the Fleet Admiral, watchful of the magi. Across from Vander, Manny swayed in exhaustion, worn out from his double duty. Vander looked to the Fleet Admiral.

"May we be allowed to return to our quarters? I understand that you will wish to question us, but the Healer and I need rest. We need to recover our strength."

The Fleet Admiral nodded tersely. "Master Lefellus and the Guards will escort you back. I will send servants to tend to your needs, but I expect you to stay confined to the room. I do not know what is going on here and I will have to trust that you mean us no further harm. But my trust is wearing thin, mage. Very thin. Should you offer the slightest resistance, they have full leave to use deadly force."

Vander inclined his head in acknowledgment. "We will explain everything after we have recovered, that I promise. And I can assure you… we are too tired to offer any resistance at all."

Kasai helped the War Mage to his feet, while nearby Lukas did the same for Manny. Aleister, now very much recovered, but silent and withdrawn, scooped up the limp form of his *liya* and cradled her to his chest. He followed behind Vander numbly, paying no attention to anything other than the comatose mage in his arms, and the form of Vander before him.

Aleister cringed inwardly, terrified of how close he'd come to losing her. It had been an odd sensation, the loosening of his own spirit from his body in the face of no physical injury. The Fox now better understood Kalla's dislike of the chains a magisterial bond placed on the magister.

They finally arrived at the room and Aleister started to kneel and lay Kalla upon her pallet, but Vander stopped him. The Fox came out of his reverie and looked into the War Mage's weary face. The mage gently touched him with one hand and Kalla with the other, using magick to scour the blood from their clothes. He waited until Aleister had settled down beside Kalla, curled protectively around her, then touched the Fox again, putting him to sleep also. With a sigh, Vander shifted and curled in a ball next to the sleeping pair. He hadn't bothered setting shields. What would be the point, if the Guard could break them?

It was odd, he mused, that he should be the one taking care of Kalla, so often had their roles been reversed. It had been a terrible shock, when she had been injured. He'd honestly thought nothing could ever hurt her. She was Amaraaq after all. She was the Empress of Wolves.

* * *

The Fleet Admiral had summoned Ventaal from the *Kujata*, still in port. She sought answers, first and foremost how it had come to pass that these magi had entered Argoth in the first place. A part of her was relieved in a way. She had never trusted the Rang'moori mage. Less so after he'd encouraged Sykes to replace Sir Lukas with James. The young Guard had already seemed very much the mage's man. Nor had she been pleased at Grosso's urging to put the Empire's military might to use and conquer Evalyce. It had only been the Fleet Admiral's own stubbornness that had held that plan at bay, hers and the *se'tovs'*. It would take much for either them or her to go against the Emperor's direct order, but that he'd not yet given, Holly be thanked.

Sykes was doing well, so said the Clerics. He'd come 'round briefly, before falling back asleep. The Magi had retreated to their room to recover, guarded by two of the Magisters. She wondered at their motivation. The female had destroyed the Emperor's ring, the one Grosso had given him, and in doing so had somehow injured Sykes. Yet they had healed him, in the end and the Admiral thought that must have been their plan all along. She wondered how they had known what would happen and wondered why Grosso had come and stolen Sir James' body away. Surely the Praetor was dead, with a great hole ripped through his chest. She'd seen the work it had taken to heal the wounded Mage.

Until Sykes recovered, the Fleet Admiral was at the helm of the Empire. She had appointed another of the Guard, Lukas' second, temporarily in charge of the Guard. If the Admiral had her way, it would be Sir Marcus who took up the mantle of Praetor permanently, as it should have been before. In addition, she had summoned Masters Parda and Elius from their stronghold in Telemachis. Their guidance would be well appreciated.

She was puzzled, too, over the enigma of the male Dashmari. She knew enough of Dashmari culture to know that he should not have survived long enough to become a Kanlon candidate. She didn't understand that, how a people could kill their children born differently. Even stranger was the man that must serve as his magister, for he wore the clothing of the Harriers. Stranger still was *how* the group had come to possess an Argosian ship. She had since learned that it was the same ship that had come to Argoth several months ago, captained by an

Arkaddian magister who served an Argosian mage, one Kalla by name. Two Arkaddians, yet the only female was Dashmari, not Argosian. Too many puzzles, not enough answers.

A soft knock at the door roused her from her musings and Owyn entered, with Ventaal behind him. The Castellan bowed to her and departed, leaving the *Kujata's* Admiral to face his superior.

"Fleet Admiral," he said with a bow of his own. The Admiral was wary and worried about the Emperor, and about Kalla as well, for the mage wasn't with Admiral Ryansdottr. He had been given no information when summoned to the Palace other than the Emperor had been injured. He had taken that to mean that Kalla and Vander had been successful.

"Admiral Karlgraffsson, *what* is going on here? It was your ship that brought these people here. And it was your ship that requested permission for the same strike-fighter to come to Argoth several months ago. A ship accompanied by a red wyvern. To all outward appearances one might think you were a traitor, Admiral, aiding assassins."

"Yes, it is the same ship. Yet I spoke honestly. You do have the Dashmari ruler here and they *do* wish nothing more than friendly relations with Argoth."

"What I have here are three magi, a wounded Emperor and a dead Praetor. One whose body was stolen by yet another Mage."

"Sir James is dead?" Ventaal asked.

"I can only assume he is dead. He took a bullet to the chest at close range. Grosso stole his body away and disappeared. None of the Guard have been able to find hide nor hair of him. For that, at least, I am grateful. Now maybe the Emperor will listen to reason. But that is beside the point, Admiral Karlgraffsson."

"No, I spoke truly. The Empress of Wolves sought to free Emperor Sykes from Grosso's influence. They disguised themselves as what Grosso expected to see, else he would have kept them from getting close to the Emperor."

"*Empress?* The only female Dashmari is a mage. Magi cannot rule a country. It is forbidden."

"It is also forbidden for magi to influence politics, yet we have tolerated the Rang'moori here for how long? Her story is not mine to tell. All I can say is that she challenged Emperor Kartoff in a bid to free the Dashmari and prevented them from attacking the Crannogmarch and Kymru. Grosso is bent on causing war on Evalyce, and to that end he had corrupted the Dashmari and even the Khan Arkaddia. Kalla freed both from his influence and now she has done the same for the Lord of Leaves. Grosso is a pawn of Al'dhumarna, an agent of chaos."

"Then why have the Harpers brought us no word from the Kanlon, warning us of this rogue mage?" the Fleet Admiral asked.

"I cannot say, Admiral Ryansdottr. Perhaps they have been intercepted. There has been rumors of Harpers disappearing of late." He paused for a moment. "Fleet Admiral, if you truly believe that I would willingly betray the Emperor then please, have me taken to the Golden Court. I do not regret the choices I have made, in playing along with Kalla's deception.

Tabitha sighed. "No, Ventaal. I will keep you here and let the Emperor make that choice when he wakes. I will have the Castellan escort you to quarters."

"As you wish, Fleet Admiral. But first, can you tell me how fares the Emperor? And Lady Kalla?"

"The Emperor sleeps. The Clerics say that he is doing fine. The magi sleep also. Lady Kalla was injured, grievously, shot by the Praetor. She would have died, if not for the red-haired one. I know not by which names to call them now."

Ventaal sank into a chair at this news, his features struck by a sudden sadness. "How? How could the bullets have harmed her?"

"Grosso gave the Guard bullets that could penetrate magically crafted shields, much to the displeasure of the Technomancers. It backfired on him, though, when he came to collect Sir James' body. The Harrier and Lukas used the rifles against him.

"Sir Lukas is now a magister in his own right, saved by a young Healer named Manny kyl'Malkador. It has come to my understanding that the outpost soldiers had been told not to let him come to the Golden Court. Emperor Kartoff collected him along the way.

"He's a lucky man, Lukas is. I am glad the mage came along when he did. Sir Lukas was doing his job as he saw best, I see that now. He didn't deserve to die for it. It was a good thing, too, that the other Healer was with them, else the red wolf would have had to make a choice- the Emperor or Lady Kalla," the Fleet Admiral replied.

"Vander. His name is Vander kyl'Solidor. His magister's name is Kasai, once of the Khan's Harriers. Her magister is Aleister Balfear, also called the Sky Fox."

The Fleet Admiral nodded. "I will call Owyn now. I'll let you know as soon as any of them are awake, Emperor and magi alike."

King Holly

Kalla groaned, stirring awake. Soreness assailed her, mostly in her chest. The smell of thriving, growing greenery tickled her nose and trees cloaked in silvered moonlight greeted her when she opened her eyes.

The Healer swayed as she stood, dizzy and disoriented. Scraps of memory came fluttering back. She had destroyed the Emperor's ring as planned, but she had been injured before she could work on Sykes.

The Praetor had shot her, bullets ripping through the shields, collapsing them. From the tatters of her memory, Kalla knew Vander had healed her. She hoped the Emperor had survived as well.

Kalla blinked muzzily, rubbing grit from her eyes. They widened slightly as she took in her surroundings. Beyond the trees, flickers of blue light winked, here one moment, gone the next. She knew this place. Someone had roused her from much needed sleep, tugging her weary spirit along on yet another journey.

But who would bring her back to the Deep Forest, and why?

Turning a slow circle, the Healer gasped as she found herself face to face with Gasta. The Keeper was cast in opal, frozen in a crouch, muzzle stretched out as if reaching for something. Tears slipped silent down her cheeks as Kalla reached a shaky hand out to stroke the Keeper's cold opal muzzle. The Healer still found it hard to believe Gasta was gone, yet here was proof beyond doubt.

Ice shivered down her spine as she recalled the day the sabre wolves had attacked, forcing her foolish attempt to teleport Aleister and herself all the way to the *Stymphalian*. A soft chuff drew her attention and she looked up, peering into the forest depths. Beyond the trees, the darkness itself seemed to writhe.

An inky form ghosted out of the forest, resolving into a jet black fox the size of a horse, with nine fluffy brushes. The fox trotted through the clearing and came to sit beside Gasta's frozen form. Sly amber eyes full of mischievousness regarded the Healer. The eyes were so like Aleister's in his fox form that Kalla guessed this must be Inari. His father. She dipped her head.

"Greetings, Fox King."

"*Greetings, Lady Amaraaq,*" Inari said. "*Please, come with me.*" The fox knelt in clear invitation.

Kalla reached out and twined her fingers in the *kitsune's* ebon fur, pulling herself astride his back. Guessing that she had been pulled into the journey courtesy of Inari, she looked around, expecting that others might be joining her.

"No others, my Lord Inari?" she asked as the fox jogged off into the Forest.

"*Not this time, Great Lady. I would ask, however, that you bring my son back to me before you depart Argoth. Others of you will have business in the Forest before all is said and done, and I would see him once more, now that he can better appreciate all that he is.*"

"As you wish, Lord Inari." She paused a moment. "Tell me, is there any way to free Gasta?"

"*That task is not yours, Lady Amaraaq,*" Inari said.

Kalla frowned at his words, then hissed in surprise as the energy of an invisible boundary pricked her skin. They entered into another clearing, this one diffused with soft green-tinged light. Royal Pines and Imperial Holly ringed the clearing, overshadowed by immense Sequoia Roi, the tallest trees known on De Sikkari.

Inari stopped in the middle of the clearing and sank down so Kalla could slip from his back. The Fox King sat his haunches beside her and waited expectantly. Neither had long to wait before a figure seemed to step from the largest Imperial Holly to border the clearing.

The figure was tall, well over seven feet. His skin, such as it was, was a mottled greyish-brown, and resembled the bark of the tree from which he had appeared. A mane of hair, darker grey than his skin, had holly leaves and berry clusters interspersed throughout. He wore pants and tunic of a deep, dark green, tiny hollyleaf patterns decorating the edges, and upon his head was a leaf crown cast of mythril. Grey-green eyes glittered with hidden mirth.

This was King Holly, the dominate of the two primary Argosian deities during winter months.

"*All is One,*" Holly said.

"One is All," Kalla replied.

"*As Above.*"

"So Below."

"*Thus are All Connected!*" they said together.

"*Welcome, Empress of Wolves, twice-born of Argoth. Welcome, daughter of the Forest. I thank you, for saving my people from a fool's folly. The Forest Empire is strong and secure. There is no need for war, and that you have stopped.*"

"*I would ask from you that which only you can do, Lady Amaraaq. If you would be so kind to free my brother and I,*" King Holly said, his smooth, soft voice floating through her mind.

Kalla nodded. "That I can do, if you will but tell me how."

More figures glided from the trees. Foxes, some black like Inari, others red with black paws and ears like Aleister, came to cluster at the Fox King's feet. All of them had two or more fluffy brushes, though none as many as the King himself.

Squirrel-like creatures the size of cats, with over-large ears, scurried across the clearing. They were *kodama*, forest spirits, and Kalla marveled to see the shy creatures. Despite all of her trips into the forest she had never see any of the *kodama*. One scrambled up her clothing, to perch precariously upon her arm, and deigned to allow her to pet its silky grey fur. Gems shone from the forest spirits' brows, rubies and emeralds glittering in the soft light. With the *kodama* came the dryads, the spirits of the trees themselves. Some looked male and others female, they were neither, truly, for trees were both male and female and neither.

One of the dryads, a slender female, guardian of a holly, stepped up to Kalla and handed the Healer a set of fox-flutes. She graciously accepted the offering, thanking the beautiful tree spirit, who gave her an enigmatic smile and joined the others at her King's side. Kalla gave King Holly a puzzled look.

"I am sorry, Great One. I do not know how to play the fox-flutes."

Holly reached out, touching her forehead where the crescent markings were, and in her mind Kalla heard the Song she must play and the manner of its playing.

"*You know all you need, to play the Song of the Trees. At your request, the High Clerics will grant you access to the Sacred Grove here in Imperia Argosia. When they hear you play, they will remember it.*"

"I thank you, Great One. I will do as you ask, as soon as I may," she said softly.

"*And I thank you, Lady Amaraaq. Sleep now and recover your strength,*" Holly said, as Kalla's grip on the journey realm began to fade.

"And remember, bring Prince Kaze back to the Forest!" Inari's words were the last she heard before things faded altogether.

* * *

Vander blinked, finding himself in the Grove of Gasta. Before him was the frozen form of Gasta himself, muzzle still outstretched where the guardian had touched the foolish young mage on the forehead, forgiving him even as the enchantment took hold. This dream was a familiar one, born of deep guilt. What he had done here had been a terrible crime, worthy of the harshest punishment.

The War Mage sank to his knees with a sob. Of all the memories Kalla had seen, this she did not know. He cringed to think of how she might react if she did. He hugged himself, slumped at the statue's feet, struggling against the tightness in his throat.

Vander wished there was something he could do to free Gasta, to restore the noble Keeper to life. Any price would be worth paying to rectify one of the greatest mistakes he had ever made.

"Any price, little wolf?" a soft voice asked. Vander snapped his head up, focusing on a shadowed figure walking towards him.

The being was tall, a towering giant of a man, yet Vander knew he was no mere man. His skin was pale grey, rough-looking, like tree bark. A mane of hair, dark green in color, had oak leaves and acorns interspersed throughout. He wore pants and tunic of a deep, dark green with tiny oak leaf patterns decorating the edges and upon his head bore a leaf crown cast of shimmering gold. Bright green eyes somberly regarded the kneeling mage. Vander bowed his head to the ground before the being who could be none other than King Oak, the Argosian deity of spring's rebirth.

"Any price, Great One," the War Mage whispered.

"Truly?"

"Yes, Great One. I would pay any price to fix this mistake, if there were a way to do so."

"*There is a way, little wolf. He is not gone, merely petrified. He can be set free, though you might not like the price.*"

"How, Great One?" Vander asked.

His heart grew heavier as he listened while King Oak told him what he must do to free Gasta. The price was a harsh one indeed, yet it was one Vander was willing to pay.

"I will do so, Great One," he said softly.

King Oak gave him a penetrating look, then nodded in satisfaction.

"*I do believe you will. Sleep now, young one. Remember your commitment when you wake once more.*"

Evergreen Palace, Imperia Argosia, Argoth, Year of the Mythril Serpent, 2014 CE

Aleister woke slowly, but made no move to rouse himself. Kalla was still sleeping peacefully beside him, her head resting against his shoulder, and he had little desire to move. He smiled to himself, remembering the first time she had fallen asleep thus, within the Deep Forest. His grin turned wry, recalling her fearsome reaction to be woken.

Grey light filtered into the room, brightening by the second. As his eyes adjusted, he was surprised to find the red frost wolf curled up beside Kalla. Well, Vander didn't surprise him. The surprise was Kasai who, in his harrier form, was wedged between the wolf and Kalla.

Aleister's smile deepened. Kalla seemed to attract people. People changed by being around her. He had seen it in Vander, in Kasai, even in himself.

The harrier stirred to wakefulness, fixing a bright accusing eye on Aleister. The Fox grinned as Kasai yawned, then jerked his hand away as the hawk snapped his beak at it in irritation.

Kasai carefully edged away from them before willing himself to change. Aleister frowned as he noticed that his Mage clutched a pair of fox-flutes to her chest.

Aleister kissed her on one fluffy ear and gently moved away to stand himself. From the balcony he heard soft voices. Looking out, he saw that Sir Lukas and Manny were already awake. He nodded towards the balcony. Kasai nodded back, and they padded softly out, careful not to disturb the sleeping magi.

"Good morning, Lord kyl'Malkador. Sir Lukas," Aleister said, nodding to each in turn. The hawk echoed his greeting.

"Good morning, Prince. Good morning, Master Kasai," Manny responded. Aleister winced at the title, but let it be.

"I checked on Lady Kalla and Lord Vander when I woke. They rest peacefully and should wake soon."

Aleister breathed a silent sigh of relief at the news.

Manny paused for a moment to look out at the rising sun, staining the sky orange and rose, before he continued.

"I was surprised to find Vander such a capable Healer, despite what I learned from Lady Kalla. He did a superb job, such that even Lord Hauss could not find fault. I wonder if she has become as skilled a War Mage as he is?"

The Fox shook his head. "I don't know, Lord kyl'Malkador. She has been given no reason, as yet, to test that."

As they waited for the others to waken, or the Argosians to summon them, Manny quizzed Kasai of life on the Plains, and Aleister of life elsewhere. Aleister smiled to himself, thinking how very sheltered the young mage seemed. He knew that novice magi rarely left the Kanlon, and never so without the company of a maester, a Mage that had earned Kyl' as part of their name.

Finally he became aware of Kalla stirring and hurried back inside in time to help her up, the others following behind. She frowned at the fox-flutes, but said nothing regarding them as she tucked them safely away. Their noise was enough to wake

Vander and the wolf huffed grumpily, stretching out his paws. With a sigh, he shifted and immediately turned his attention to Kalla. His look was one of relief when he saw that she was up and about.

"You gave us quite a scare yesterday, Dashkele," he said. She favored him with a warm smile.

"You did a good job," she replied, assessing her own body and the healed damage. "But what of Emperor Sykes."

"He is well. Lord kyl'Malkador saw to that. Our cover is blown of course. The Fleet Admiral was none too happy. ...And Sir James is dead, at least as far as we know. Grosso took his body away before any could make sure," Vander replied.

"He did take a shot to the chest at close range. Grosso doesn't seem to be near as skilled in healing as any of you. Surely he couldn't have healed the Praetor," Kasai said.

"Grosso is not," Vander said softly. "But if the Nagali had a use for Sir James, he could very well have used the Artisan as a conduit." The War Mage shivered, recalling his own experiences. Al'Dhumarna had still found him useful after he had taken out Gasta and had thus deigned to give Vander a tiny fraction of power, but that tiny bit had been enough to allow the War Mage to teleport himself and Shingar out of the Forest with no ill effects, a feat he would otherwise have been unable to pull off.

A soft knock on the door interrupted them. Without waiting to be acknowledged, Cleric Eddasson walked in, flanked by two of the Guard. The young Cleric beamed at them.

"Good. You are all awake and looking well. The Emperor would like to see you," Zacharias said.

"The Emperor fares well?" Kalla asked. The Cleric nodded.

"Indeed he does, no thanks to the young Lord kyl'Malkador here. And your own efforts, milady. He would like to see you as soon as possible. If you will please come with us." He turned to exit, then looked back at Kalla again, eyes full of hidden laughter. "And the answer to your question is yes, milady, as soon as we may."

Kalla frowned at the departing Cleric and followed him out the doors. The others filed in behind her, with the two Guard taking up the rear. They were taken not to the conference room this time, but to Sykes' own quarters. More Guard were posted around the doors. They gave the group of Magi an assessing look, still not sure how angered they should truly be. Zacharias knocked on the door, and at a soft command from within, led the group into the room.

Sykes sat in a chair surrounded by a number of people- High Cleric Morgansson, the Fleet Admiral, Sir Marcus, now dressed in the uniform of Praetor, and, to Kalla' surprise, Admiral Karl-graffsson. The Emperor looked weary and careworn. He cast a look towards the newcomers, his dark blue eyes tired and thoughtful. He rose heavily to his feet and bowed graciously to her.

"Lady kyl'Solidor. Or should I call you Lady of Wolves?" At her shocked look he smiled and elaborated. "The High Clerics have told me all about who and *what* you are. Admiral Karl-graffsson has confirmed what he could. I thank you, Lady, for freeing me from Grosso's influence.

"It feels... it feels as if I have been half-asleep this whole time. And to think, I ignored the counsel of those I should have most trusted." Sykes paused, looking to Sir Lukas. The Magister met his gaze unflinching. "You have my apologies, Sir Lukas, for ever doubting your loyalty. Glad I am that young Lord kyl'Malkador came along when he did."

"I did what I felt needed to be done, Your Grace. I'm only sorry that I didn't succeed." Lukas replied.

"People make mistakes, Your Grace. The point is what you learn from it. All's well that ends well, as the Arkaddians are wont to say. It's a good philosophy," Kalla said with a sly look at Kasai. The hawk scowled at her a moment, before returning the grin.

"As you say, all's well that ends well. The Lady is right, Your Grace. You are alive, as is Sir Lukas. Grosso is gone, along with his influence. You did not end up in an unnecessary war," Kasai said.

"I'm glad to see you chose Marcus to replace James. He will serve you well," Lukas said softly.

"Yes, I have little doubt of that, Sir Lukas," Sykes said sadly. He turned his attention back to Kalla. "Great Lady, what reparations would you have of me, to repay our discourtesy?"

"You owe no such reparations. But, we were in earnest when we said that Dashmar seeks an alliance with Argoth. Both would benefit, I should think. It is true that Dashmar is full of a great many natural resources. The Wolf People have little use for metals or gems. What they do have need of is the availability of more food. Life in the mountains is harsh. I would have it be less so," Kalla said.

"Very well, Lady Kalla. Shall we return to the conference room? I think breakfast would be in order before anything else," Sykes said. She nodded and followed as the Emperor and his people left the room. She fell in step beside Ventaal.

"I am glad to see you are well, Kalla," he said softly.

"Thank you. But, Admiral, what are you doing here? You must have gotten in some time last night."

"Aye, the Fleet Admiral summoned me. She wished to know how it had come to pass that I had let you through the borders in the first place. I do not know yet what the Emperor will choose to do with me," Ventaal replied.

"What did you tell them?" Kalla asked.

"The truth. I told them the truth. That I let you through knowing full well that you were magi, but that it was also truth that the Dashmari ruler wished to seek an alliance with Emperor Sykes. My actions were treason, though I would not change them for anything. More good than bad came from it, no matter what happens, but at the very least I should be stripped of my command."

"And the worst?" Kalla asked quietly.

"Exile. Or at the very worst, execution."

"I'm sorry, Ventaal, that you should be punished for helping us. I don't think it will come to that, though. Emperor Sykes is not that cruel."

"I don't regret it, not at all. No, I doubt it will come to my execution either, but..." his voice trailed off as they arrived at the conference room. The Admiral gestured for her to enter and followed behind. Their seating arrangements were much altered this time, with Kalla where 'Kartoff' had been seated and Aleister in her spot, followed by Vander and Kasai, then Manny and Sir Lukas. Marcus occupied Sir James' spot. There was a great deal less tension with this meal, a great deal more bantering conversation.

The Castellan and his servants brought in a meal of eggs mixed with mushrooms and sausage and apples from the Palace's cold cellars. As they ate, Kalla managed to coax from Zacharias how they had learned of who she truly was. Apparently she wasn't the only one to have received a visit from the Tree Lords that night. She was a little concerned though, at how quiet Vander was during the meal. He spoke little and seemed preoccupied.

The meal was finished and the room once more became a conference room. Kalla spent the rest of the morning in negotiation with Sykes and together they reached an amiable agreement. Argoth would be allowed greater mining rights in Dashmar, in return for imports of much needed foodstuffs. Kalla had requested that Admiral Ventaal and the *Kujata* be sent as the Argosian emissaries. She had been pleasantly surprised when Sykes agreed with no fuss. Ventaal had been just as surprised. As late afternoon approached, Emperor Sykes sent Owyn off to have two copies of the trade agreement drawn up. They stood to stretch and Zacharias spoke up.

"Perhaps now would be a good time to retire to the Grove. The others may come as well, if they wish," he said.

"Now is as good a time as any." She looked to the rest of her group. "They will come. It is fitting that they should be there," she said. Aleister and the others gave her quizzical looks, but said nothing aloud as they followed Jonas and Zacharias through the Palace.

"*What is going on, milady?*" Aleister asked. Briefly she told him of her meeting with King Holly and of his request.

"*Ah, that explains where the flutes came from then. I had wondered,*" he said, laughter bubbling in her mind. The Fox found it amusing and was delighted to learn that they would be going back to the Forest.

"*Never thought I'd see you happy about going into a forest,*" *Kalla* responded with laughter of her own.

At the center of the Evergreen Palace stood a great grove of trees, surrounded almost completely by a clear moat of water. This grove was the seat of the Clerics' power, the heart of Argosian spirituality. The grove was open to the sky, the waters channeled from the nearby Algassey River, entering through one section of the Palace and exiting another. Kalla recalled overflying the Palace with her father, when she was much younger. The Evergreen and its grove were breath-taking from the air. From above one could see that the Palace was laid out in a series of concentric, spiraling circles of green granite interspersed with the elegant tree towers. At the center of the rings had stood a majestic grove of Regal Oaks, sharing space with Royal Pines and Imperial Holly.

Kalla grew still as she entered the grove, crossing over the small bridge that spanned the burbling river. This place felt as the Deep Forest did. Immeasurably old and sacred. Without being told, the group stopped at the fringes of the trees, even the

Clerics. Kalla paid them no heed, as the Song began to fill her blood. Settling herself at the base of an immense oak, she closed her eyes and began to play.

Time stood still, or so it seemed to the Fox, as his mage played. He saw that the others were as captivated as he was by the haunting music. A slight rustling sound joined the sound of flute and water. Aleister's breathe caught as he realized that the noise came from the trees themselves. The branches swayed gently, though there was no breeze here to cause such and it seemed to him that if he didn't look directly at them, he could just make out the forms of androgynous figures *within* the trees.

A sensation of being watched prickled his sharpened sensitivities and it was without surprise that he found there were now *kitsune* all around the grove. Most stayed on the fringes of the trees, across the way from the Emperor's group. A few came as far as Kalla and two even came to where he stood, watching him with sly, knowing eyes.

The Healer's music wound to a close and as it did so the trees rustled louder, then stilled suddenly. As if it were a cue the *kitsune* darted away, disappearing into the darkness and safety of the trees. Kalla opened her eyes slowly. She could feel the difference in the air and knew that she had been successful. The Tree Lords were free now, to act once more in this realm.

We thank you, Lady Amaraaq, a voice whispered in her mind, the sound of leaves in the wind.

She smiled. *You are welcome, Great Ones.* The Healer rose to her feet and walked to where the others stood. Looks of awe greeted her and there were tears damp on the cheeks of a few, Vander and Sykes among them. She frowned, looking at the War Mage with sharpening concern. He looked more withdrawn now than he had earlier.

"That was beautiful, Lady kyl'Solidor," the Emperor said softly, pulling her out of her thoughts. "I did not know you played the fox-flutes."

"I do not, Your Grace. This is the one and only time. I thank you for the compliment though," she said with a small smile and handed the flutes to Zacharias. The young Cleric reverently wrapped them in a forest green cloth he had brought with him. The young Cleric departed with the flutes, leaving them in Jonas' care. The elder Cleric led the small group back to the conference room, where Owyn now waited with the trade agreements. Kalla and Sykes looked them over before each signed both sets of documents. Kalla tucked her copy into her robes and touched fist to heart.

"I thank you, Emperor Sykes. I truly believe that both our peoples will benefit from this."

"And I, you, Empress Kalla. I have no doubt that we can learn from one another,' Sykes responded, returning the gesture.

"Indeed. By your leave, Emperor, I will prepare a message to Aryff, Dashmuynin of the Blood Wolves. In the absence of myself or Vander kyl'Solidor, it is Aryff who serves as Regent," Kalla said. Sykes nodded and Owyn went to retrieve paper and quill for the Healer. When she finished her letter, Kalla sealed it and turned it over to Admiral Karlgraffsson, with the admonition to send it ahead of the flagship.

The evening wrapped up with a nice dinner of roast duck, giant *belligrassi* olives from Southern Argoth stuffed with sharp vykr cheese, potato dumplings and acorn bread with rowanberry jam. Kalla sighed and sat back, fully contented.

"Emperor Sykes, may I ask an indulgence of you?" she asked. Sykes brow creased and he gave her a questioning nod.

"I wish to travel to the Deep Forest. There is business that the Prince and I have there, at the Temple of Inari. I request permission for myself, Aleister, Vander, and Kasai to travel thus. Lord kyl'Malkador and Sir Lukas as well, if they so wish. Vander can serve as Manny's mentor for learning to work with Lukas.

"The Forest is not safe at this time, Lady kyl'Solidor. Gasta… the Keeper seems to have lost his influence. Nothing binds the sabre wolves and other forest spirits," Sykes responded. Vander flinched at the Emperor's words.

"That will not be a problem, Your Grace. Once there, Lord Inari can give us what protection we need, though I doubt that the forest spirits will bother me," she said.

"This is true. Very well, permission granted."

"Thank you, Your Grace," Kalla said. She turned to Manny and Lukas. "Will you join us? I promise you will find no better mentor than Vander here. The travel will do you a world of wonder, Manny. You need to get your feet wet!" The Healer exclaimed with a sly grin. Manny returned it with a sheepish one.

"I would be honored to travel with you, Lady Kalla."

"Well, that's all settled then. I will have proper mounts and equipment readied for you. How soon would you like to depart?"

"I see no reason why it can't wait until morning, Your Grace," Kalla said.

The rest of the evening the group spent in relaxing. They were lead back to the Emperor's private quarters, where more soft chairs had been arranged, along with a round table. Sykes challenged Kalla to a game of *kessala,* which they all eventually joined in, even Vander and Manny after they gained confidence. The *kessala* game finally wore down after a fair amount of gains and losses on everyone's part.

Chigali boards were produced and the magi and magisters pulled their pieces out. Much to Kalla's surprise, both Lukas and Sykes knew how to play and in short order the Emperor had retrieved a finely crafted set of forest green pieces and another of autumn orange. It seemed that the strategy game had been a love shared by the Emperor and the former Praetor. Sykes ran a nostalgic hand over the orange pieces before turning them over to Lukas.

"These should go with you, my friend," he said sadly. Lukas gently took them from the Emperor.

"I thank you, milord. Looks like I may find a good use for them. Give this young pup here a run for his money, I might," Lukas drawled. Manny gave him an indignant look, earning laughter from the rest of the group. The young Healer gave up and joined in.

Kalla faced off with Sykes first, leaving Aleister to face Vander and Manny to face his own magister. The others watched intently and Kalla sensed that Kasai had picked up the game quicker than even Aleister had. When the bouts were finished he asked to face Kalla. Sure enough, the hawk had learned enough to keep her on her toes, though he accepted his loss gracefully. Kalla turned her pieces over to Zacharias, so that the Cleric could learn. The arrangements shifted again, with Zacharias facing Lukas, Manny against Sykes and Aleister against Kasai.

The first two battles were over quickly, leaving the two magisters still facing one another. Both were holding ground quite nicely, neither quick to give up territory or advantages. The pair played cautiously and Kalla had the feeling that there was more to it than simply enjoying the game. It was a bit of sibling rivalry, the brothers testing wits with one another. She watched, thoroughly amused, as each grew more frustrated.

The game drug out, passing a half hour, then an hour, before it was finally decided in a draw. Though the brothers congratulated each other heartily, and accepted compliments for a well-fought game, she could still sense the hint of rivalry behind it.

A discrete yawn brought Aleister's attention to her and soon enough Kalla and her group found themselves back in their quarters, with the Emperor's assurances that all would be ready for them to depart in the morning. Sykes turned his remaining set of *chigali* pieces over to Kasai, a gesture which touched the hawk far more deeply than he let on. The Healer assumed that there would be many more *chigali* bouts between the brothers before all was said and done.

It took Kalla only a few seconds to fall asleep, safely wrapped in the Prince's arms. One by one, the others fell asleep. All but Vander, who lay awake, tossing and turning, restless with his task to come, yet grateful that he would not have to part company so soon from Kalla. Guilt wracked his thin frame, guilt and shame for his past and guilt for what must inevitably happen to his new magister. Vander would gladly pay the price needed to free Gasta, but he sorely wished that Kasai needn't pay it with him. However, what would be, would be. The War Mage finally shifted form and crawled near enough to press against Kalla's leg, where he soon joined the rest in slumber.

Penance

Kalla sighed and shifted in her vykr's saddle. A feeling of déjà vu swept over her as they approached the town of Millan. The lights from the Dancing Bear Inn twinkled merrily in the deepening purple of twilight. Kalla stopped before the inn and slid from the shaggy beast's back, as several stableboys swarmed out to take their vykr. The Healer smiled as Pip ran up to her.

"Welcome back, Lady Kalla!" He frowned at her for a moment. "You look different, Lady Mage. You have puppy ears. Are you in disguise?"

"Hello again, Pip." Kalla grinned. "You might say that, little one," She waved an open palm through the air as if plucking something from it, then fanned coins out from her closed fist. "You know the drill, young one. Take good care of our vykr and you get another when we leave." She placed one in the hand of each of the clustered stableboys, watching their eyes widen. A chorus of *dos mere* greeted her and the boys trundled off with the animals.

Wylsin hurried forward, his face lighting up with recognition. A look of puzzlement flitted across his face momentarily as he took in her new look, but he made no comment on it.

"Welcome back, Lady Mage, Master Balflear. You will be staying the night with us again?" he asked.

"Yes, Master Wylsin. We've a large group this time. Do you have five rooms available? And dinner in the dining hall would be a blessing," Kalla replied.

"Yes, Lady Mage. We have more than enough rooms this night." Wylsin's voice trailed off as he caught sight of Vander behind her and the innkeep's face grew cold and distant, but not before he gave Kalla a brief questioning look.

"I think you will find Lord kyl'Solidor a much changed man, Master Wylsin," Kalla said, soft enough that only Wylsin and Aleister heard her. The innkeeper's face softened and he nodded.

Kalla glanced over her shoulder at the Dashmari and found him still withdrawn and distracted, as he had been since their escapade healing Sykes. Vander caught her gaze and blinked slowly. His eyes widened as recognition of the place hit him. Sorrow flitted across his face, followed by shame, but the War Mage buried these things as he gently pushed past her to face Wylsin.

"Master Wylsin, when last I was here, I did you and yours a terrible injustice. I would apologize for my behavior and make what amends I can," Vander said. Wylsin gave the thin Mage a measuring look. A moment's more consideration and Wylsin offered the War Mage a cheerful smile, noting that his customers were attending the group without seeming to pay them any mind. Wylsin's reaction ensured that the others would take no offense to the mage's presence.

"Apology accepted, my Lord. Actually, there is something you can help with, if it be in your power. Yours or the Lady Kalla's. We have two housed here who have been attacked by sabre wolves. The beasts have grown more brazen. I know not why Gasta no longer keeps them at bay, but they have wandered this far from the Deep Forest and now attack travelers in broad daylight. Our physicker has done what she can, but the wounds have infected and they burn with a terrible fever. There is not a military facility or Technomancer Lab this far in. Another mage has seen them also, but she was no Healer. She has done what she can for them."

Vander hissed out a frustrated breath,

"Yes, Master Wylsin, I can help them," he said.

"We can help them," Kalla corrected gently, but the War Mage shook his head.

"No, Dashkele, it is my responsibility." He looked to Wylsin, "Please, show me where they are."

Kalla frowned at the determination in his voice. She wasn't sure why he felt the need to take it all upon himself, but if it would help him to make amends in his own mind she wasn't going to deny him that. He was more than capable of healing them both, of that she was very certain.

Wylsin gave him another measuring look, surreptitiously gesturing for one of the servants. He gave them soft instructions to take the mage to the sickrooms and to take Vander's pack to his room. Kasai started to follow him, but halted abruptly at the mage's unspoken request to remain with the others. More servants hurried up to the group to relieve them of their packs, as Wylsin herded them to a table.

Soft music filled the dining area, keeping the voices to a low murmur. Kalla was surprised to find that the source of the soothing music was a Harper, his fingers lightly dancing across the strings of a round-bellied mandolin, an instrument from Ne Ramerides. She studied the man a moment. His skin was noticeably paler than average, even in the inn's low lighting. Amber-brown hair fell past the high collar of his tunic, matching the neatly trimmed beard on his face. Unless the Healer missed her guess, the Harper himself hailed from Ne Ramerides. As they were seated, he ended the purely orchestral piece and began another, adding a rich singing voice to the music. The song he sang was a mournful tale of a valiant hero, his battle with a fierce dragon, and his ultimate betrayal by his closest of friends.

"Something to drink, my Lord and Lady Mage? Magisters? Fury wine, perhaps," Wylsin asked with a wry grin. A chorus of affirmatives answered him and the innkeep bustled away to the kitchens. Within moments, flagons of fury wine had been set before the group, along with platters of roast goose, potato dumplings, apple and almond salad and warm brown bread fresh from the ovens, dripping butter.

They ate quietly, content to listen to the Harper and to watch the crowd. Only Kasai was tense, the absence of his mage leaving him uneasy. After a time Vander returned, weary and once more withdrawn. His patients were doing fine now, resting peacefully. He had been able to eradicate the infection and close the wounds of both. Wylsin brought food and fury wine for him, which the Dashmari gratefully accepted.

Now that Vander was back among them, Aleister and Lukas were able to lure Kasai away to a nearby table where a game of *kessala* was in progress. The three were readily accepted among the players. Kalla took opportunity of the quiet and withdrew her journal. She sighed at the sense of familiarity, yet this time was different. This time it was not just her and her newly acquired magister. This time it was her and a whole group of people that she couldn't ever have imagined traveling with.

The Healer reflected on the changes of the past several months and found herself thankful for the people she had been drawn together with. Not just Aleister, as both her magister and her *liya,* but for Vander, with all the changes that had been wrought in him, for Kasai, though she regretted the why of it, for Manny, the young Malkadoran Healer, even for Sir Lukas, though he and his mage were the newest of her traveling companions. She was most thankful for the fact that they had managed to save the former Praetor. Manny had chosen well, she thought. He would find no better protection.

Beside her, Manny followed her example, pulling out his own journal. While they wrote, Vander finished his meal. Pushing the plate aside, the War Mage rested his head on his arms. His eyes were closed, but the occasional swiveling of his ears betrayed the fact that he was not asleep, but in fact paying close attention to everything around him. He shifted and sat up as soft footsteps approached their table.

"Greetings, Lady Kalla."

Kalla looked up as another Solidoran mage stopped by their table. The Lady had short black hair that curled around her face and the sea-green eyes of a Sevfahlan regarded them intently. The new mage leaned heavily on an ornate cane, crafted to look like twin serpents twined around one another. From the way she stood, the cane was no mere accessory, but a necessary instrument.

Behind her were the Harper and a woman Kalla guessed was her magister. The magister had the bronzed skin and tawny colored hair of the Persiali, from a land far beyond Ishkar. The woman moved with the elegance of a hunting cat. Though she wore no armor, a curved sword was belted at her waist and a slender, spike-headed mace hung opposite it. Kalla's mind scrambled for the mage's name. With it came the realization that the cane *was* necessary, for a magickal accident had rendered the leg barely useful and not even the Healers could fix it.

"Greetings, Lady Justina," Kalla said. She gestured towards the empty chairs. "Please, join us. I must admit, I didn't realize that the 'other mage' Master Wylsin spoke of was still here."

Justina gracefully slid into a seat across from Kalla, Harper and magister following her example. Kalla smiled slightly as Aleister's curiosity brushed against her mind. She assured him that all was well and he turned his thoughts back to the game. Justina nodded towards Vander and Manny.

"Greetings, Lord Vander, Lord kyl'Malkador. May I introduce Harper and Cara, my magister."

"Harper...?" Kalla asked, her tone asking for the man's name as well as title.

"Just Harper. The man refuses to give me any name to call him by. Just as he refuses to quit following me around." Aggravation laced her words and Justina threw the man a dirty look. He merely grinned back at her and the woman named Cara laughed. Kalla frowned as she caught a glimpse of a thin, woven slaver's collar around the man's neck, mostly hidden by the high collar of his tunic. The Harper was obviously no slave, so why did he wear a collar, she wondered. Recalling rumors of Harpers disappearing, she put voice to her question. The man's face grew somber.

"It is true. The slavers have grown bold. They attack even the Harpers, when they find us. Justina found me in a slaver's camp. She and Cara made short work of the slavers and freed the slaves. I owe her a life-debt, according to the customs of my people. I wear the collar to remind me of that debt. Until it is paid, I belong to Lady Justina and have no name save that which she gives me. Thus, I am destined to merely be Harper for she will give me no other," the Harper said with another grin.

Kalla had guessed correctly. The man hailed from Ne Ramerides. She had heard of the Rameridean custom of a life-debt and she could certainly respect the man's dedication. The Healer did find it disturbing to find the rumors confirmed. If the slavers would go so far as to attack Harpers, what else might they dare?

"What brings you to Argoth, Lady Justina?" Kalla asked.

"We were seeking new Kanlon candidates. The Technomancers have already departed back to the Academy. Between us we found seven in the region with the gift. Two will be going back with me," Justina said.

The Technomancers of Argoth belonged to the military and were among the few gifted of magick who were not tied to the Kanlon. All Argosian children who were found to be gifted were given a choice- to either serve the Empire as a Technomancer or to go to the Kanlon and become a magi. Kalla herself had been given the same choice.

Justina turned an appraising eye to Vander. The older mage had been at the Kanlon when Kalla and Vander had departed and knew, too, the skills of each. She hadn't missed that it had been Vander and not Kalla that had disappeared with the innkeep's servant.

"Lord Vander-," she began, but the War Mage shook his head.

"Just Vander, Lady Justina. Just Vander," he said softly. As if anticipating what Justina were thinking he continued, "And yes, I did go to heal the wounded Master Wylsin is caring for."

Justina raised her eyebrows in a questioning look. "I wasn't aware you were a Healer, Vander."

"I was not, Lady. It is thanks to Kalla that I have that gift now."

Kalla leaned forward, explaining things to Justina. The Sevfahlan looked thoughtful.

"How interesting. Do you think you could recreate such a bond? It would be immensely useful to transfer skills in such a way. And apparently combining such unusual gifts with one another lends a greater level of innovation in using them. I don't think there is a Healer at the Kanlon with a Defensor's full training."

Kalla thought for a moment. She shared Justina's reasoning, the link she and Vander shared and the talents gained were immeasurably valuable. The Healer pondered for a moment longer, letting her thoughts sharpen into focus. The more she considered it, the surer she was that she *could* recreate the bond.

"I am fairly certain that I can. I don't think it would have to be maintained that long, either, not among fully trained magi. A day at most. I don't think, however, that it would be wise for a mage to learn the gifts of more than two others, ever. The strain would be too great," Kalla said.

"Well, why not try now. There are four of us here, if young kyl'Malkador wishes to try as well. By your reckoning, you and the War Mage can share gifts with one other person and you are the only ones to have shared such a bond. I am an Artificer by training, with Artistry as my secondary skill," Justina said.

"Very well," Kalla replied. She looked to Manny and the young Healer gave her a slow nod.

"I will try," he said. Vander echoed his agreement.

"There are four of us. I see no reason why all of us should not try," Kalla said. After a few moment's discussion, it was decided that she would share with Manny and Vander would bond with Justina. Briefly, she shared her intentions with Aleister.

"*Do you think that wise, milady?*" he asked. Kalla assured him that everything should be fine. From Vander's expression, she gathered that he had gotten a grumpy response from Kasai, but the hawk did nothing more than glance over his shoulder from the *kessala* table. Kalla decided to start with Justina and Vander and reached a hand out to each of them. They slipped their hands into hers and she focused her intentions and slowly wove a bond between the two magi, carefully recreating the one she had shared with Vander. When she was satisfied, the Healer sat back and withdrew her hands from theirs.

"I... do believe it worked," Justina said. "I can feel another presence in my mind."

"As can I," Vander said. Emboldened by this success, Kalla stretched her hand out to Manny and the young Healer took it with some trepidation. It wasn't that he didn't trust her. More that this was all so strange to him. He was still learning to deal with the bond he shared with Lukas. Kalla took a moment to make sure that Aleister or Kasai one had told Sir Lukas what they were attempting, then wove the bond between them. It took less time the second go round and sure enough, she soon felt a new presence in her mind.

Kalla had learned a great deal during the forging of the new bonds and the Healer was certain that she only needed to work with one half of the pair to undo it, so she and Justina could part ways the next morning. The magi conversed amongst themselves a bit longer until a tug on the back of her robes turned Kalla around. Several of the children she had entertained before had clustered behind her, along with a handful that must have been Justina's charges, for she saw children from Rang'moori, Kymru, and Zinlin among them. Some gave Vander nervous looks, though the Dashmari certainly looked more approachable now.

"Will you tell us stories again, Lady Mage?" one of the Argosian children asked shyly.

"Certainly, young one," Kalla said. She turned her chair around as more children, emboldened by the others' success, gathered around her. From the corner of her eye, Kalla saw Aleister stand from the *kessala* table. The Fox had withdrawn with his winnings, more eager to hear Kalla's tales than to keep playing. Kasai and then Lukas withdrew and wandered back over to the table, pulling up extra chairs beside their magi. Kalla settled into her storyteller mode, well aware that her audience had grown beyond just the children.

"Once, long ago, there was a Healer who, along with a Seer, was called in to tend a man believed to be possessed. Through the Seer it was determined that the spirit was a young *kitsune*. The fox spirit had become trapped in the man's body quite by accident.

"*I didn't mean to harm anyone. I just came looking for something good to eat. You didn't have to shut me up like this!*" the fox said plaintively, through the Seer. As she sat talking with the Healer, the Seer drew a small, glowing ball from within her robes and began to play with it, absent-mindedly dancing it across her knuckles. The orb was the *kitsune's* fox-ball, for as you know, all *kitsune* have them.

The people present thought the ball pretty enough, but they believed that the Seer had brought it with her, hidden away to trick them, for you see, not all the people present believed that the man was really possessed. Many thought him to be faking it, merely for the sake of attention. The Seer began to toss the ball in the air and one young man, braver than the rest, dared to snatch it out of the air. He quickly tucked it into his own pocket.

"*Confound you!*" the fox cried. "*Give me back my ball!*"

The man ignored the fox's pleas to return the orb, until finally it said tearfully, "*You do not know how to use the ball. To you it means nothing, but to me it is a terrible loss. By the One, if you do not give it back I will be your sworn enemy, but if you will but return it to me, I will be your protector and guardian.*"

The young man still believed the whole thing to be a sham, but his interest in the affair was waning.

"*So if I return it, you'll protect me, huh,*" he said.

"*Yes, yes. I swear it. By the One, I swear it,*" the fox replied.

"*Very well,*" the man replied. He gave the ball back to the Seer, which made the fox very happy. The Healer then dismissed the *kitsune*, wherein it left quietly. No sooner than the Healer had done so, then the people seized the Seer and searched her, seeking the orb. They did not find it and had to conclude that she and the patient really had been possessed by a fox spirit.

Some time later the young man was returning home after dark from a visit to town. When he reached a section of forest he began to grow nervous, for the area was known for bandits. Terrible visions of being attacked and robbed ran through his head. It was then that he remembered the *kitsune* that had vowed to protect him.

"*Fox! Fox! I need your protection now,*" he said softly. A series of sharp yips came out of the darkness in answer and suddenly there was a fox there on the path before him.

"You kept your word after all, fox. I'm touched. I wish for you to protect me as I travel home. Bandits are said to be in these woods and I am afraid to travel any further alone."

The fox seemed to understand. It went on before the man, keeping a sharp lookout and avoiding the usual path. The man followed behind the fox. Finally, it stopped and arched its back, before moving on again, with ginger steps and extra caution. The man took the cue and began to tiptoe along behind the fox, closely following its path.

Soon the man heard human voices and through the dense trees he now traveled through, he caught sight of the shapes of a large group of men. As he passed near he overheard what they were discussing. They were bandits planning their next robbery! The fox had led him on this odd path, a way that no normal man would ever use, just because the bandits would expect no one to pass so close to them. The fox disappeared once the young man was safely home.

Thereafter, the man called upon the fox often, sometimes for protection, other times merely to talk. The fox remained faithful to his vow and always came when called. More and more touched by the fox's faithfulness, the man was glad that he had had the good sense to return the fox-ball to the *kitsune*."

Kalla finished her tale with a sly glance at Aleister. The Fox gave her a mischievous grin in return. Without missing a beat, the Healer launched into another story, one of a wolf eager to gobble up a red-cloaked girl, then moved on to a story of Inkanata, where a young boy encountered a band of thieves and a trapped djinn. She wrapped up her session with a tale from Kymru.

"Long ago, time beyond knowing, when the world was young and the Great Ones still walked freely among men, it came to pass one day that Pryderi, lord of Dyfyd and his closest of companions were reminiscing. A great battle had been fought. Fought and won, yet the cost had been great. Many of their friends and companions had been lost. Yet of those that remained, each had a home to return to, a family waiting to greet them. Each that is, except Manawydan, son of Llyr.

"*Alas, among all those gathered here, I alone have no place to return to,*" Manawydan lamented as the pair sat talking on a hill overlooking the army encampment.

"*Lord, be not so heavy-hearted. Your cousin is king of Raven's Rock. Surely he would welcome you in his home?*"

"*Nay, my friend. My cousin and I do not get along well. I would not be as welcome there as you might think.*"

"*Well, then, my friend, will you listen to some advice?*" Pryderi asked.

"*I will do so. What advice to you have?*" Manawydan replied.

"*The seven cantrevs of Dyfyd were left to me, when my father passed. My mother, Queen Rhiannan lives there still. I will give her to you, along with authority over the seven cantrevs. These are the finest cantrevs in the land! The title to the land will remain mine, but I am content that it be you and Rhiannan who enjoy it and if you so desire territory of your own, well then, that you shall have as well.*"

"*I do not desire that, my friend,*" Manawydan said. "*but the One reward your friendship.*"

"*The truest friendship I have to offer shall be yours, if you wish it.*"

"*I do wish it, friend. May the One reward you. I will go with you to Rhiannan and the cantrevs of Dyfyd.*"

"*Well said, my friend. That is the right thing to do,*" replied Pryderi. "*I do not imagine that you have ever yet seen a woman so beautiful as Rhiannan, nor one with such a sweet, musical voice. It is a voice to charm the very birds, I tell you.*"

The pair set out next day with the army marching home. As they passed town by town their ranks dwindled, til at last it was only Manawydan and Pryderi. Finally they reached the realm of Dyfyd and were greeted by Rhiannan and Cygfa, Pryderi's young wife. Both were overjoyed that Pryderi had returned home safe and sound. Rhiannan and Cygfa prepared a feast for the returning heroes and at the feast Manawydan sat close by to Rhiannan and the two lost themselves in talk. Gradually Manawydan's thoughts and desires grew tender for her. It came to him that Pryderi had not lied- Rhiannan really was quite beautiful.

"*Pryderi, my friend, I will accept your offer,*" Manawydan said, turning to Pryderi.

"*What offer?*" Rhiannan asked.

"*Lady, I have given you as wife to Manawydan ap Llyr,*" Pryderi said.

"*Gladly will I accept,*" she said.

So it was that the homecoming feast became a wedding feast and before it had ended, the couple had slept together.

They finished the rest of the wedding feast and then set off on a tour of the cantrevs of Dyfyd so that Manawydan might get a good sense of the land. They hunted, fished and enjoyed themselves. Manawydan had never seen such a bountiful land and was touched once more by the depth of Pryderi's friendship. And a friendship grew fast between all four, so that none wished to be without the others at all.

The travelers returned, wherein they set up another feast at Alberth, the chief seat of Dyfyd. When the meal was concluded, the companions went to the outskirts of Alberth to Gorseth Alberth, a great grassy hill near to the capital. As they were sitting on the mound, talking of idle things, there came a sound such as thunder rumbling. With an especially loud burst of thunder mist descended over the land hiding the companions from one another.

The mist finally lifted, but what the companions found was not the last things they had seen before the dismal fog. Where once their flocks and herds roamed, now there was nothing. Gone were the huts of the people and even the people themselves. The only things spared was the royal court behind them. Only the four companions remained, in what was now a desolate, forbidding landscape.

"*By the One, what has happened to everyone and everything? Let us go and look,*" said Manawydan. They returned to the hall and found nothing. They searched the kitchens, the cellars, the towers, the chambers and the sleeping quarters, but still no sign of people did they find. They then went looking across the countryside, but it, too, was desolate. When their searching turned up naught, the four returned to the court at Alberth. They spent their days feasting, hunting and exploring further and further away, though they still found no people.

They enjoyed themselves and let the years slip by. First one, then a second. At length they grew tired of the monotony and decided to do something other than merely remain in Dyfyd.

"*Let us go into Rang'moori and seek a trade by which we can support ourselves,*" Manawydan said.

And so they set out for Shrockshire within neighboring Rang'moori and there they set up a saddle-making business. They soon excelled at their chosen profession and before long no one would buy a saddle or pommel if they could not be gotten from Manawydan's shop.

When the other saddle-makers realized that the only business they were receiving were orders that Manawydan could not fill they grew jealous and formed a conspiracy to kill their rival and his companions. By lucky chance, the group received warning and decided to leave town before that unhappy fate could come to pass. The four made for another town, far from the previous one.

"*And what craft shall we take up here?*" Pryderi asked.

"*We shall make shields,*" Manawydan replied.

"*But we know nothing of shield-making,*" Pryderi protested.

"*Nevertheless, we shall try it,*" his companion replied.

So it was that they set up a business as shield-makers and before long, as before, no one would buy a shield if it could not be gotten from Manawydan's shop. And as before, their competitors grew jealous and conspired death to their rivals. The companions learned of these plans and fled to yet another town.

"*And what craft shall we take up here?*" Manawydan asked.

"*Whichever of the two we have done before,*" Pryderi replied.

"*Nay, we shall try a new one. We shall be shoemakers.*"

"*I do not know anything of making shoes,*" Pryderi said.

"*Well, I do and I shall teach you,*" Manawydan replied. "*Shoemakers are not bold enough to kill us nor forbid our working.*"

So it was that the companions took up the craft of shoemaking and before long there was no one in the town who would not buy shoes unless they could be gotten at Manawydan's shop. Despite their initial thoughts, the shoemakers did indeed band together and plot the death of their rivals. Once more the companions learned of these plans and once more they decided to flee. However, this time they decided to return to Dyfyd. Though their journey was long, they at last reached home and there kindled a fire and began to support themselves with hunting and such farming as they were able. They spent a month or so assembling a hunting pack from those dogs that had been left behind at the court. A year passed thus.

One morning Manawydan and Pryderi rose and prepared to go hunting. They made ready the dogs and set out from the court. Some of the dogs ran ahead and entered a small copse which was nearby. Moments passed before the dogs quickly retreated, shaking with fear. As Pryderi and Manawydan approached the trees a shining white boar with red ears burst forth from it. At the hunter's urging, the dogs gave chase. The boar would stand at bay against the dogs until the men approached. Then it would retreat and so the chase continued until the boar led them to a great stone fortress which the men had not seen before, though they had passed this way many times. The boar and dogs disappeared into the fortress. The men remained on a mound before the fortress, striving to hear the barking of their dogs, but only silence greeted them.

"*Lord, I will go and see what has happened to our dogs,*" Pryderi said.

"*The One knows, that is not a good idea,*" Manawydan replied. "*This building has appeared from nowhere and you should not enter it. Doubtless, the ones responsible for the enchantment of this land have caused the fortress to appear.*"

"*The One knows, I will not give up my dogs. We need them for hunting,*" Pryderi replied. Ignoring Manawydan's advice he rode forth into the fortress. Once inside he found neither man nor beast, but only a fountain with marble all round it and a golden bowl fastened to four chains set over a marble slab. Captivated by the beauty of the gold and the craftsmanship of the bowl, Pryderi walked over to touch it. No sooner than his hand touched the bowl then he found himself stuck fast, unable to move or speak.

Meanwhile, Manawydan waited patiently for Pryderi's return. Day turned to evening and still his companion had not left the fortress. Finally he decided to return to the court. As he entered, Rhiannon looked to him and asked, "*Where is your companion and where are the dogs?*", wherein he told her the whole story.

"*The One knows,*" she replied, "*You have been a bad companion and lost a good one.*" With that she set out for the fortress. When she arrived she found the gates open and nothing concealed. Entering, she found Pryderi were he stood, stuck fast to bowl and stone.

"*Alas, my son, what are you doing here?*" she cried. Then she too reached out to touch the bowl and likewise became a statue even as Pryderi was, unable to move or speak. When night full fell, thunder rolled across the land and a dense mist descended over the fortress. It vanished and they within with it.

When Cygfa, Pryderi's wife, found that she and Manawydan were alone in the court she became afraid, though she had known him for many years. Noticing this, Manawydan said, *"The One knows, you are mistaken if you weep for fear of me. I swear that you will find no truer friend than I and no harm will come to you from my hands. Between the One and myself, even were I still in the prime of my youth, still I would be loyal to Pryderi. For your sake too, would I be true, so do not be afraid."*

"The One knows, that is what I was hoping to hear," Cygfa replied and she took comfort in his words and grew more cheerful.

"Well, we cannot stay here. We have lost the dogs for hunting. Let us return to Rang'moori. It will be easier on us there," Manawydan said. Cygfa agreed and so the two found themselves once more in Rang'moori. Manawydan again took up the craft of a shoemaker. After a year had passed, it came once again that people would buy no shoes if they could not be bought from Manawydan's shop and again he and his companion found their lives in danger. Frustrated, the pair returned to Dyfyd, this time bringing with them a load of wheat.

They once more settled in the court of Alberth and, though it was hard at first, they soon began to support themselves with such fishing and hunting and planting as they could. With the wheat Manawydan sowed first one croft, then a second, then a third. The wheat flourished under his loving care and soon it came harvest time. Seeing that the wheat was ripe he said to himself, '*I will reap this tomorrow.*'

The following morning he returned to the first croft with the grey dawn, only to find the wheat gone. All that was left were the broken, stripped stalks. He marveled at this and went to check the other crofts. Finding them still safe and moreover, just as ripe, he resolved to reap the second one the next day, but when he returned to the croft the following morning he found it to be just as the first had, stripped and broken.

Checking the third croft once more, he found it still intact. *'Shame on me,'* he thought, *'If I do not stand guard this night. Whoever destroyed the other crofts will certainly return to complete their work this night. I will watch and find out who it is.'*

Manawydan gathered his weapons and set himself to watch the croft. Towards midnight he heard a great uproar and, looking out, saw an immense host of mice, numberless as the stars of the heavens. Before he could do anything, the horde swept down upon the croft and began to carry off the ears of wheat, leaving only broken stalks behind. Angered and dismayed, Manawydan rushed in among the mice, but he could no more focus on a single one than if they had been gnats. One mouse, he noted, was slower and heavier than the rest. He chased it down and caught it. Thrusting the squirming creature into his glove, he tied the opening shut and returned home, where he hung the glove up on a peg.

"*What is that, Lord?*" Cygfa asked.

"*It is a thief I caught stealing from me,*" Manawydan replied.

"*What sort of thief is it that could fit in a glove, Lord?*" she asked, wherein Manawydan told her the whole tale of how the mice had come and ruined the crofts.

"*One of them was very heavy and I have caught it; it is now in my glove and I will hang it tomorrow. By the One, had I caught them all I would hang each and every one!*"

"*Lord, that would not be strange,*" Cygfa said, "*but it is hardly proper for a man of your rank to be handling that sort of creature. Do not bother with it, rather let it go.*"

"*Shame on me if I did not hang them all- but I will hang the one I did catch,*" Manawydan said.

"*Well, Lord, there is no reason I should plead for its life, save to prevent your being dishonoured; therefore do what you will.*"

The next morning Manawydan set out with the mouse. Reaching to Gorseth Alberth he began to construct a tiny gallows. As he did so, he saw a scholar coming towards him along the road, dressed in old, worn clothes. This disturbed Manawydan for this was the first person other than his own companions to have been seen in Dyfyd in many a long year.

"*Lord, good day to you,*" the scholar said as he drew near.

"*The One be good to you and welcome. Tell me, where are you going?*" Manawydan replied.

"*Lord, I come from Raven's Rock. Why do you ask?*"

"*Only it is that there have been no other people save myself and my companions in this land for the past several years, not til you have shown up just now,*" Manawydan said.

"*Well, Lord, I am merely passing through on my way to my own country. But what sort of work is it you are about?*" the scholar asked.

"*Hanging a thief I caught stealing from me.*"

"*Lord, what sort of thief. The creature I see in your hand is but a mouse and it is scarcely fitting for a man of your rank to be handling such a beast. Let it go.*"

"*Between the One and myself, I will not. I caught it stealing and I will punish it appropriately.*"

"*Lord, I will give you this* sork *I received in alms if you will but let it go,*" the scholar said.

"*Between the One and myself, I will not let it go, nor will I sell it,*" Manawydan replied.

"*Very well, Lord, do as you like. If it did not seem degrading to me to see a man of your rank handling such a creature I would not trouble myself,*" the scholar said and went about his way. Manawydan continued his work, but soon enough another traveler came down the road. This time it was a monk riding a shaggy vykr.

"*Greetings, Lord, and good day to you,*" the monk said.

"*The One be good to you and welcome. I would ask your blessing,*" Manawydan replied.

"*The One's blessings upon you, Lord. What sort of work are you about?*"

"*Hanging a thief I caught stealing from me.*"

"*Lord, what sort of thief. The creature I see in your hand is but a mouse and it is scarcely fitting for a man of your rank to be handling such a beast. Let it go.*"

"*Between the One and myself, I will not. I caught it stealing and I will punish it appropriately.*"

"*Lord, I will give you three* sork *if you will but let it go,*" the monk said.

"*Between the One and myself, I will not take any price in place of what it deserves, which is to be hanged,*" Manawydan said.

"*Very well, Lord. As you will,*" the monk said and rode off. Once more Manawydan set about his work, drawing a string about the mouse's neck and preparing to hang it, when a priest came down the road. The priest stopped near his work.

"*Priest, I would ask your blessing,*" Manawydan said.

"*The One's blessings upon you,*" the priest said. "*What sort of work are you about?*"

"*Hanging a thief I caught stealing from me.*"

"*But is that not a mouse I see in your hand?*" the priest asked. "*Here, I will give you seven* sork *if you will but let it go. It is not seemly for a man of your rank to be seen destroying such a worthless creature.*"

By this point Manawydan was growing angry with the constant questioning. He did not know why it should be this day, of all days, when people should finally decide to travel through his deserted realm, nor why they should care so much about his business.

"*Nay, I will not let it go,*" he said.

"*If you will not let it go for that, I will give you twenty-four* sork. *See here, I have it now,*" the priest said.

"*Between the One and myself, I will not let it go, even for twice that amount. I have no use for money.*"

"*As you will not take that, I ask you to name your price,*" the priest said.

"*I wish for the return of Rhiannan, my wife and Pryderi, my close companion,*" Manawydan said.

"*You shall have that.*"

"*Between the One and myself, that is not all.*"

"*What else?*"

"*The removal of the enchantment over the cantrevs of Dyfyd.*"

"*You shall have that also, only free the mouse,*" the priest said.

"*Between the One and myself, I will not. I wish to know what this mouse is to you.*"

"*She is my wife- otherwise I would not ransom her.*"

"*How is it that she came to me in this form?*" Manawydan asked.

"*Plundering. I am Lloyd the Sorcerer and it is I who enchanted the cantrevs of Dyfyd.*"

"*To what purpose?*"

"*In revenge. Pryderi's father disgraced and dishonoured my brother. When my company heard you had returned once more to this land, they asked to be changed into mice in order to destroy your crops. On the third night, my wife and her ladies asked also to be changed and this I did. My wife is pregnant. Had she not been you would not have caught her.*

"*I will give you Pryderi and Rhiannan and I will lift the enchantment from Dyfyd. I have told you who the mouse is- now release her!*" Lloyd exclaimed.

"*Between the One and myself, I will not,*" Manawydan said.

"*What more do you wish?*"

"*I would have your promise that there will never again be any other enchantments cast upon Dyfyd.*"

"*You shall have that. Now release her!*"

"*Between the One and myself, I will not.*"

"*What else would you have?*"

"*Your sworn word that no revenge will ever be taken on Pryderi, Rhiannan, Cygfa or myself, nor any of our descendants, because of this,*" Manawydan said.

"You shall have all that you have asked for. The One knows, that last was a good thought, for otherwise harm would have come upon you," Lloyd said.

"Yes, I figured as much. That is why I protected myself," Manawydan replied.

"Now release my wife!"

"Between the One and myself, I shall not. Not until I should see Pryderi and Rhiannan before me."

No sooner had he spoken than Pryderi and Rhiannan appeared. Manawydan greeted them, overjoyed to see them safe and sound.

"You have all that you have asked for. Now sir, free my wife," Lloyd said once more.

"Gladly," Manawydan replied and set the mouse down. It ran over to Lloyd and the sorcerer struck it with a magick wand, turning it back into the loveliest young woman any had ever seen.

"Look around you and you will find all as it once was," Lloyd said as he and his people disappeared. They looked and found the dwellings, people and animals restored and the land once more flourishing and never again was Dyfyd troubled by any kind of magick.

Kalla bowed to her audience, earning applause and the crowd began to disperse.

"You would make a fair good Harper, Lady Kalla," Harper said. She inclined her head to him.

"Thank you," the Healer replied, working to stifle a yawn. She knew Aleister was getting sleepy and from the new link she shared with Manny she could tell that he, too, was drowsy. Beyond that she could vaguely sense his Magister, though it was nothing to what she, Vander and Aleister had shared. Wylsin himself lead them up to their rooms. Kalla smiled to herself- the innkeep hadn't missed the rings she and Aleister wore, nor the fact that she had asked for five and not six rooms. Accordingly, he had put their stuff together in the same room.

Though Justina had parted ways the very next morning, Kalla was pleased to find that she had guessed correctly, and was able to break all of the bonds easily. Her group continued on its way towards the Deep Forest, with Vander teaching Manny and Lukas how to work together. They came across more victims of sabre wolf attacks and in each case, Vander insisted on taking care of it himself.

Towns gave way to wilderness. Each night from there on out, the magi set up reinforced wardings. Though they saw the glow of the sabre wolves' blades at night and heard them all around, the creatures never bothered the travelers.

"Inari, Fox King, guide our steps that we might reach the Temple once more and reach it in safety. Open a path for us, Fox King and let our journey be swift and unfettered," she cried out in Argosian. The trees before them seemed to shift with a sigh and a path revealed itself. Kalla took the lead and rode down the path.

Wolf's Honour

The Fox King's magick led them to the clearing Kalla and Aleister had stayed during their previous sojourn to the Deep Forest. After the camp had been set, she and Aleister departed for the Temple, assuring the others that they would be fine and would be back as soon as possible. As when they had entered the forest to begin with, they crossed a boundary line just beyond the campsite and found themselves before the Temple of Inari.

The Forest had eradicated all traces of their previous visit. All that remained were a handful of vykr bones and the broken vines that Aleister had pulled free of the doors. New growth had already taken their place.

Aleister freed one door of its vine covering and tugged it open. He gestured for her to go through first.

"After you, milady."

Kalla gave him a wry grin and walked through. Conjuring magelight globes, she set them to dancing before her as Aleister entered the Temple. They had gone no more than a few feet into the gloom before they crossed another boundary line and found themselves in the Temple's inner courtyard. The brightness of the full moon shone down upon them, reflecting from the pool in the center. Across the way, Inari watched them with amusement.

Welcome back, my son. The giant fox dipped his head low to the ground. *And I welcome you to my humble home, Lady of Wolves. Thank you for taking the time to return here.*

"You're welcome, Lord Inari. Thank you for letting me through this time."

Inari chuffed softly as he walked towards them. *Indeed.* Bright eyes fixed on her. *You have brought my son far, Lady of Wolves, just as you yourself have come far. It is time for both of you to claim all that you are.* With these words the Fox King blew a cinnamon scented breath over the pair.

Kalla staggered, suddenly dizzy. The locks to Amaraaq's power shattered. Aleister caught her and she heard his breath catch in his throat. He buried his face in her mane, inhaling the scent of myrrh and she became acutely aware of his desire. Inari disappeared, his laughter fading in the night, leaving the pair alone in the moon-swept courtyard. The burgeoning power of the wolf goddess crashed over her, pulling both of them under in a tidal surge.

Deep Forest, Argoth, above Evalyce, Year of the Mythril Serpent, 2014 CE

Vander scrubbed a hand over his face and sighed. Manny and Lukas were finally asleep. He had hoped that Kasai would go to sleep as well, but the hawk was prowling the camp's shielded perimeter.

"*Where are you going?*" he asked as Vander started to pad away into the darkness.

"*I'm… going for a walk,*" the War Mage replied.

"*Of course you are. Because every sane person goes for a walk in the middle of a dark, hostile forest, in the middle of the night.*"

"*Kalla and Aleister left. What makes you think I would be in any more danger than they are,*" Vander objected. Kasai waved away the notion.

"*Can't say I think either of them are very sane right now, but that's their business. You are mine. I'm coming with you.*"

Vander shrugged, walking off into the gloom. Behind him, Kasai muttered something in Arkaddian as he followed his mage into the trees. It didn't take long before they reached Gasta's grove. Vander took a deep breath and forced himself to go stand before the frozen form. He lifted a hand, as if to touch the outstretched muzzle. Vander let his hand fall, gesture aborted, and conjured a warding that cut Kasai off from him.

"*What are you doing?*" the hawk growled.

"*What is necessary. I made a terrible mistake and it must be corrected.*" Vander glanced over his shoulder at Kasai, who *I am sorry.*"

"*Sorry for...?*" Realisation tightened the hawk's voice. He pounded on the ward. "*No! Don't...*" Muted light rippled from the impact, illuminating the clearing. "*Vander, let me in!*"

Vander ignored Kasai, and turned back to Gasta. In a fluid motion he withdrew the longtooth knife that Aleister had given him and drew the sharp blade across his own throat. The War Mage sank to the ground, blood spattering against the opalescent statue and pooling at its feet.

Time seemed to stand still for Vander. He heard a dull thud as Kasai crashed to the ground, the magister's voice a weak protest in his mind.

"*Forgive me. Great Lady, please forgive me...*" he thought as darkness threatened to overtake him. He became aware that the statue above him was shifting and rippling as stone gave way to living flesh once more. With a deep sigh, Vander gave in to the darkness.

* * *

Vander stirred weakly at the sharp crack of power near him and suddenly he found himself lifted, cradled close to a body that smelled of rowan, a scent he should have known but couldn't place.

"What have you done…" a gentle voice said. A golden pulse of energy flooded through him. It wasn't the coolness of a Healer's touch, but a brightness and heat that healed his wounds, restoring and rejuvenating him. As quickly as it had come, the power was gone and he became aware that it was Kalla who held him tight, gently rocking him, sobbing softly. His magelight had vanished and the War Mage couldn't see her.

"Lady Kalla…?"

She stopped and loosened her grip on him. "Vander, why? And where is Kasai?" she asked. He shut his eyes again as magelight illuminated the clearing once more.

"Nice tail," a voice rasped behind her.

"What?" The Healer blushed furiously at the realisation that she had no clothes. Releasing the War Mage, she conjured her clothes about her. Vander sat up slowly, nausea roiling in his belly.

"I'm fine by the way," Kasai muttered. "I enjoy dying. It makes me appreciate living all the more. Now answer the Lady's question, if you please. What the hells were you thinking?"

"I-" Vander began.

He did it to free me, Lady Amaraaq.

Kalla flinched at the voice. She turned, and drew in a deep breath as she found herself face to face with a living, breathing Gasta.

"But… why?"

"Because it is my fault that Gasta was gone. It is my fault that the sabre wolves have left the confines of the Forest. When I was here last, it was at Al'dhumarna's behest, to put an end to the Guardian of the Forest and create chaos," Vander said softly. "The night I healed you at the Palace, I ended up here in a dream journey. King Oak came to me and told me of how I might free Gasta, of how I might correct the greatest mistake I have ever made. The price was a fair one. My life in return for the Keeper's. My only regret was that Kasai would have had to pay the price with me."

Your lives would not have been forfeit, Gasta rumbled. *If Lady Amaraaq had not intervened, I would have healed you myself. It was enough that you were willing to make that sacrifice, young wolf. I forgave you before. I do so again and I thank you for being willing. I knew before that it wasn't in your heart to do as you had. Glad I am to see you free of those chains, cubling.*

"How did you manage to keep such a burden from me?" Kalla asked. Vander was silent a moment, head bowed. He raised his head to look at her and his eyes widened when he saw the mark upon her brow. He quickly bowed his head again.

"Dashkele, you bear the last mark. You are Amaraaq. You are Mother, Lady, and Empress."

A series of sharp yips forestalled her reply as Inari arrived. Aleister sat astride the huge fox's back. The night had changed him as well. Fox ears poked up through his hair, and he had three fluffy tails the same russet color as his fox form. Kasai's previous comment took on a whole new meaning. Patting the back of her robes, the Healer found that she had a tail of her own to match her ears, another change wrought by Amaraaq's power. At least he had the sense to dress before leaving the Temple.

"Nice tails," Kasai said in a wry voice.

"What?"

"You heard me. Nice tails," Kasai repeated. Vander and Kalla started to laugh at the Fox's puzzled expression.

"Aleister, you have fox tails now. Three of them," she said. They laughed all the harder as he turned a circle trying to see and finally reached around to grab one. He looked at it with a dumbfounded expression, then looked to Inari.

"How do I make them go away?"

I'm afraid you are stuck with them, little Fox. Inari chuffed a laugh of his own at Aleister's consternation.

"And how did I not notice this before... I should think it would have been hard to miss?" he asked in a somewhat aggravated tone.

"Would now be a bad time to mention you also have fox ears?" Kalla asked innocently. The ears were black, same as his fox form. The claw earring was gone, but in its place were two small silver hoops. Aleister dropped the fox brush and ran his hands over his head, groaning at what he found.

You are fully kitsune now, Prince Kaze. The ears and tail are part of the package.

Kalla rose to her feet, pulling Vander up with her. Behind them, Kasai stood as well. The hawk shook himself, stretching, and shifted form. He fluttered to Vander's shoulder and promptly bit him on the nearest ear. The War Mage yelped in pain and winced as the harrier's claws sank deeper in his shoulder.

"*If you ever do something so foolish again without telling me, you will get worse than that. Do you think me without any honor, that I could not have understood the debt you sought to pay?*"

"*I thought you would have tried to stop me, yes,*" Vander replied. The hawk gave an indignant squawk, his feathers fluffed in irritation.

"*I'm sorry. I truly am. Don't worry, I have no other hidden debts to repay.*"

I think it is time and past for you to return to your companions. They have woken and found themselves deserted. Gasta rumbled.

Good journey til the end, Lady Amaraaq. Take good care of my son. Inari said. *And don't worry, Kaze, you look just fine.*

A panicky Manny greeted them when they arrived back at the camp.

"Where did all of you go? We woke up and no one else was here."

"We had business in the Forest, Manny. Business with Inari and Gasta."

"You found Gasta? The Keeper is alive?" Lukas interjected.

"Yes, Sir Lukas. One order of business was to free Gasta. Objective complete. The Forest should be back in order in no time at all," Kalla replied.

"That is a relief," Lukas said.

"Indeed it is. I am sorry that we had you worried. Vander didn't wish to wake you when he left. No doubt he thought he would be back before you did so," Kalla said.

She shared a look with the War Mage, swift assurance that his secret was safe.

Isle of Whispers, Year of the Mythril Serpent 2014 CE

The Nagali hissed in anger. He had lost the Arkaddian ruler and now the wolf goddess had set the Argosian emperor free as well. No matter. He was growing stronger with each passing day and the companions had yet to even visit the Elephant Lord, much less find the spear of the dark dragon goddess. His servants had kept them busy at least, scurrying around to prevent war from erupting.

Al'dhumarna thrashed in his prison and more shards of mythril fell away, revealing shimmering blue-green scales. He hissed again, this time in satisfaction. The more he freed himself, the more power he regained. Fully restored he would be near as strong as his 'sire', if the Lord of Living Nightmare could truly be called that.

Araun's gift had given him form, but it was humanity itself that had breathed life into the great Nagali, and humanity that had granted him his power. Even now he turned the Lord of Xibalba's gift back upon itself, even when Araun would have held it in check. The stronger their fear, the more it fed his dark murmurs in their hearts and minds.

From the mists of the island croaking chitters came to his ears and the island's inhabitants came forth. Always before, they had avoided his prison, but now they came to his siren call of blood and battle and now, finally, the Nagali had the strength to open the gates to send them forth into the inhabited lands of De Sikkari to wreak havoc upon an unsuspecting populace.

Fennec Nall

It was the subtle change in the thrum of the engines that woke Kalla. The thrum deepened and slowed as Aleister brought the ship to ground. Nearby, Lukas' airship, the *Heracles,* settled in its own space. The *Heracles* was a *Jupiter*-class fighter, built for a crew of three, with twice the armor and firepower of the smaller *Kruetzet*-class ship.

On the way to Port Benwick they had visited Dashmar, to see how Ventaal had fared. The *Kujata* had brought the promised supplies from Argoth, and Kalla had taken a cue from the Khan Arkaddia's book for the distribution of resources.

Ventaal's crews had already begun clearing small areas near potential mining sites. Leave it to the Argosians to clear an area with little disturbance to the surrounding forest. The trees they had culled to make room for the barracks were sent to nearby packs. Soldiers went with them and helped the Dashmari to restore or rebuild living halls and other buildings in need.

Kalla watched as Kasai slid from Thiassi's back, making his way to the ship as paddock workers swarmed out to them. They would take on supplies here and refuel the ships. The trek across the ocean was a long one, for such small aircraft. The *Hera-*

cles was nearly evenly matched with the *Stymphalian,* despite its greater size. The *Jupiter-* class, like the *Kruetzet,* was built for the pure speed of close quarter combat rather than the endurance of long distance travel. If not within the bays of one of the massive flagships, the smaller strike-fighters were transported in passage-ships that could hold a full sri-talon of ships the size of the *Stymphalian* or *Heracles.*

Kalla knew the next leg of their journey would be the longest, twelve long hours across the ocean. Vander would be traveling with Lukas for this trip. He could monitor the ship to allow the magister time to rest, though any fancy flying would need be done by Lukas himself. Kalla would spell Aleister when needed. Her greater concern actually lay with the wyvern, though they had assured her that the trip would not be a problem. The wyvern could glide much of the way, relying on the air currents.

Kymru, Evalyce, Year of the Mythril Serpent, 2014 CE

Grosso snarled wordlessly, staring down at the body at his feet. After fleeing Argoth with the injured Praetor, Grosso had managed to make it Kymru. He had a home there, hidden in the forests and well-shielded from prying eyes. He had healed James as best he could, but the man's life-force was still slowly fading. Grosso had bound him as magister and been fortifying him with what strength he could spare.

The mage tensed as an eerie barking cry erupted outside the small hut. The cry came again, closer this time, sending shivers down his spine. He wondered where

Arturo was. What had he summoned the guardian for, if not to protect the house? A sinister feeling grew, soaking into the very ground itself. Grosso's heart hammered. Sweat beaded his forehead, and he pressed back against his workbench.

He let out a small moan as a dry scratching rattled the door, like skeletal fingers against the weathered wood. The flames in the hearth blazed high, before guttering completely, extinguished by a dark magick.

The scratching came again, then the handle began to shake. A soft click and the door swung open, drawing in a sense of dread. An inhuman figure stood silhouetted in the moonlight that shone through the now open door. The barking cry reverberated through the small confines, and James stirred restlessly on his pallet.

I have sent you help. See to it that you use it well. Al'dhumarna's cold voice slithered through Grosso's mind as the figure stepped forward into the hut. The creature was tall, towering nearly seven feet, bearing a staff just as tall. A musty scent accompanied the creature, like warm dragon leather and birds. As it came through, two more followed, bearing a third between them. Grosso backed away as they lowered the body beside Sir James.

The creature crouched before the pair on the floor and leaned forward. In profile, it had a long snout. Slender fingers with two inch talons reached out to the Praetor's body.

Grosso felt James' alarm as a bright flash engulfed them. He felt James howl in his mind, and pain seared through every nerve in his body. The mage curled in the floor, giving voice to screams his magister couldn't. The pain built, like fire in the veins, and Grosso surrendered to blessed darkness.

The mage woke, sore and stiff, throat raw and parched. The shadowed creature crouched in the corner, its companions clustered around it. He reached out to brush James' mind and found his magister healed. The man's mind was different, colder, somewhat alien.

Your Magister is healed. He is still useful. Go now to Su Ramerides. This time I intend you to put a stop to the Wolf's plans once and for all. Igasi and his trith *will accompany you.* Al'dhumarna's cold voice hissed.

The mage's pale eyes widened as fire erupted in the hearth and he found himself face to face with Igasi's reptilian gaze.

Marzan Desert, Ishkar, Inkanata, Year of the Mythril Serpent, 2014 CE

Kalla watched Aleister a moment, as he stared out into the desert beyond the shields. This was the Marzan, the wild, untamed desert. The ships were grounded near some old ruins half covered in sand, brought to earth by a fearsome sandstorm that still raged beyond the shields.

"Well done!"

Kalla turned her attention from her brooding magister to find Manny with a somewhat surprised look on his face. From Lukas' slightly dazed expression, Kalla guessed that the pair had managed to mind-speak one another. She put her guess to the War Mage, who was looking positively elated.

"Yes, Dashkele. They have indeed." He gave the pair a wicked grin. "That means I can start having a bit of fun."

Manny gave her an uncertain look and she shrugged. She had no idea what the Dashmari was up to. She and Aleister had never gotten further in their training than mind-speaking one another before they had departed the Kanlon.

Kalla watched with interest as the pair joined Lukas and Kasai. The War Mage shielded them, then he and his magister fanned out, circling the pair between them. At an unspoken command both attacked Manny at the same time, one with magick, the other with drawn swords.

Vander, who had been alternating magickal attacks with physical ones, sent a fireball racing towards Manny. The young mage gestured and Kalla blinked in astonishment as it ricocheted off the spontaneously created shield and rebounded on the War Mage. A gesture on the Dashmari's part and the fire was absorbed into another protective shield.

"Very good. Your reaction time is getting quicker," he said with a bit of pride in his voice. He called a halt to the exercises and they came to join her and the Fox.

"Good work," Kalla said as they flopped down in the shade of the strike-fighters' wings. Lukas gave her a nod, but Manny fair beamed at her praise.

The magisters settled to clean their weapons. Sykes had given the two Arkaddians rifles like those of the Guard, as both had proven very adept at using them, though Kalla knew Kasai preferred his twin swords. As they tended blades and rifles, Kalla settled down to read. Vander had shifted and now dozed peacefully beside her. Time passed and Kalla grew drowsy herself. She drifted off to sleep to the sound of the magisters talking as they worked.

Sharp fox yips woke Kalla some time later. Darkness had fallen and moonlight glittered on the desert sands. More yips woke Vander and wolf stood and faced the darkness with his ears pricked forward. Aleister stood at the shield's perimeter, looking out into the night. The wolf started to trot forward, but before he had gone two paces, a flurry of foxes tumbled into the campsite, passing the wards as if they didn't exist. The foxes were the same tan color as the sands themselves, with sharper features and huge over-sized ears. Each fox had two or more tails.

Kalla recalled Arvynn's words to Aleister and guessed these must be Fennec Nall's. Sure enough, as the desert *kitsune* clustered around Aleister, a fox the size of Inari glided out of the darkness. Like the smaller foxes, Fennac Nall was dun-colored, with over-size ears, though he sported nine fluffy brushes. He stopped before Aleister.

Welcome, Prince Kaze. It has been a long time since any of our forest brethren have visited here. The fox dipped his head in Kalla's direction. *Greetings to you as well, Lady Amaraaq.*

Kalla came to stand next to Aleister, Vander following along beside her. The others had woke and slowly came to cluster behind them.

"Greetings, my Lord." Kalla said, inclining her head politely. Aleister echoed her greetings with a full bow. Nall chuffed softly in amusement.

I am glad that you took the time to visit us, Prince Kaze. You look to be managing well. I'm afraid I cannot offer you anything nearly as valuable as your sire and the Lady Arvynn have given you, but I would offer advice to the both of you.

Be careful and tread softly. Al'dhumarna's prison is failing faster than before. His influence grows stronger by the day. It is said that the Crescent Reavers have returned to the land.

"Crescent Reavers?" Aleister asked with a frown.

Aye, Prince Kaze. They call themselves the rahksa, but history and legend give them the name Crescent Reavers. And reavers they be. They are merciless. Servants of the Nagali they were before and are again. Their blood hunger knows no limits.

"It is said they are beings created by Araun's gift. Is that true?" asked Kalla.

No, Nall said. *No, they are flesh and blood creatures, among the oldest species in all of De Sikkari. The oldest and the most dangerous, distant dragon-kin. Long have they been confined to the Isle of Whispers, but Al'dhumarna is strong enough now to open the gates between here and there. He has sent them forth once more from their isolated island home. He will send them hunting after you and yours, Lady Kalla. Have no doubt of that.*

"Oh good. I can hardly wait," Kasai said in a dry voice. Nall chuffed again.

I have no doubt that you will be up to the task, the Desert King said.

"Thank you, milord. You have given us knowledge we didn't have before. That will help me keep what I value most safe," Aleister said.

Just so. I hope you will not encounter the Crescent Reavers, but I will not hold out on that hope. You have disrupted too many of the Nagali's plans. The big fox dipped another bow to Kalla. *I thank you, Lady Amaraaq, for healing the lands.*

"It was my pleasure. I hope to finish that task before long and to free the patrons of the land, if they so wish it of me."

We belong to the Elephant Lord. You go to visit him and the Lady Laeksheen already. As for the rest, you will have to visit their lands, but I am sure they would appreciate it. There are only two whose jurisdiction encompasses all lands and you have already freed them.

Kalla gave Nall a puzzled look, before raising her hand to the whistle about her neck. "They are the same..."

Aye. Nall had a grin in his voice. *They are the same. Perhaps you can help more people see that. You have made a loyal friend in the Lord of Illusions, for seeing past what you thought he was. Farewell now, Lady Amaraaq, Prince Kaze.*

Nall departed into the darkness, the smaller foxes running about him, leaving Kalla to mull over his words. She hoped she could help others to see the truth of Araun. That train of thought reminded her of her promise to Vander. She looked down at the wolf standing beside her.

"How would you like to go visit Kartoff now, my friend?"

The wolf gave a weak wag of his tail that she took to be assent. She disappeared into the *Stymphalian* and returned with her staff. The bells jingled softly as she used the tip to trace a huge spiral into the soft sand. With a touch of magick she froze the rippling shape in place, then stepped out onto it. Vander and Aleister followed her.

Kasai was a bit more tentative. Grumbling, the hawk shifted and fluttered to sit on the wolf's head. Vander rolled his eyes up to look at the bird and was promptly bit on the ear. The wolf yelped as Kalla and Aleister laughed.

The Healer looked to Manny and Lukas, standing uncertainly on the outskirts of the spiral. She gestured for them to join the others.

"There is no reason why you should not come, with all of the rest of us gone. All of you, if you wish," she said, taking in the wyvern. "The two of you shouldn't be left out of everything."

At her invitation Amaterasu and Thiassi came and coiled along the outer edge of the spiral, completely encompassing the group.

"Are you sure we can come, Lady Kalla?" Manny asked a little nervously. She smiled at him.

"I am certain," she said. Closing her eyes, Kalla whispered her request to the Master of Xibalba. Before she had even finished speaking there came the soundless concussion of power and the world blurred and shifted, the two planes overlaying one another. In the otherworld the ruins around them were whole once more and Kalla saw that they were once a temple to Azurai.

How uncanny, she thought, *that Aleister should have been led to come here of all places.* They moved off of the spiral and the world solidified.

The temple before them was assembled in giant carved stone blocks cunningly set together. Twin statues of *ghilan* clothed in flesh sat their haunches to either side of the open doorway, looking imperiously down their muzzles at the group. Xibalba itself was swathed in twilight, as if the sun were setting yet there was no sun here. Kalla lit several magelight globes and started for the doorway.

Behind you, Lady Amaraaq. Araun's wintry voice whispered in their minds. The group turned to find Xibalba's master lounging in the sands, surrounded several *ghilan* and hounds. Araun's forelimbs were tucked up under him, the skeletal wings folded at his sides.

The wyvern had uncoiled and now each dipped their heads to the ground in an elegant bow. Manny and the others bowed as well. Kalla touched her fist to her heart, bowing slightly in an acknowledgment. She wondered what the others saw him as. Manny and Lukas didn't seem frightened, merely a bit nervous. She guessed that they saw him as 'Auric' rather than the spectral being she saw.

Welcome to Xibalba. Araun said. *It has been long since any of the dragon-kin walked this realm willingly.*

We are honored, Great One. Amaterasu said. Araun chuckled dryly.

Please, make yourselves comfortable. What brings you?

"Thank you, Lord Araun," Kalla said. "I had hoped to let Vander speak with Kartoff, if that is acceptable." As she spoke a frost wolf ghosted from the dimness beyond Araun. He had cream colored fur, with socks and ears the same color as Vander's fur; a wolf that matched the hounds in color.

The two wolves stared at one another for a moment, then Kasai fluttered from the red wolf's back to Aleister's shoulder and the wolves trotted further away from the group. Aleister gave the hawk a wary look and winced as the claws dug into his shoulder.

Kalla came closer and knelt in the sand, the others following her example. "Lord Araun, how is it that Xibalba is not tied to any one land. Kituk is tied to Dashmar, the Hounds to Arkaddia, Oak and Holly to Argoth. You are not tied to any land, save your own."

I have no people either. One could say that all are my people and thus all lands are mine. I was the first of us all, born from that which is All and Nothing. I Sang the First Ones into being with my gift. Those Old Ones are gone now, returned to the ether from which they were created. Sadness tinged Araun's voice. *Only the Seven are left, of those elder gods...*

Once... it seems so very, very long ago... there was a group that believed that I was the only true Deity. Absurdity... Araun's voice grew soft as he was drawn further into his own memories.

"What happened, Great One?" Manny asked. Araun turned his burning sapphire gaze upon the young Healer.

That belief spread like wildfire, for no reason I can fathom. These people, they persecuted any who would not believe as they did. Belief in many of the First Ones and their descendants faded away. They were forgotten and so they left, returning to Shae N'Sala and eventually to the One who is All and Nothing.

These people rejected the magick of the world. They killed those who had the gift and that rabid fervor created such fear. That fear, as you can well imagine, made itself manifest and the magi were blamed. The fear and hatred grew and from it the distinction between 'Azurai' and 'Araun'.

And Araun they hated and feared just as much or more than they hated the magick-users. They called me 'evil' and so I earned the appellation 'Lord of Living Nightmare.'

"Who are these people, Lord Araun? Why do we have no records of them?"

Because it was eons ago. Long, long before the great Cataclysm that shook even the foundations of the worlds beyond the physical.

Ahh, Kalla thought. No records existed from before the Cataclysm. She wondered if they had anything to do with the strange artifacts that magi sometimes stumbled upon. Things like the song-cubes.

The world Araun described sounded terrible to her. A world where people paid honor and homage to one deity to the exclusion of all others. Now it was simply understood that each people had their own Patron deities and none were better than the others, merely different. But then, weren't all families composed of different personalities? And they were all a big family, weren't they?

"Can you tell us more?" Kalla asked.

It pains me to say… I remember little else. Little save the fact that in the end… they… ripped the world asunder. Araun's skeletal tail twitched, betraying agitation.

Kalla decided not to press further and turned her questions to something that had been tickling her mind since they had begun this conversation.

"If you were the first, who created you, Lord Araun?"

Her question earned a more heartfelt chuckle from Master of Xibalba. *Who indeed? I come from the One, as do all things. In that, all things inherently have a spark of the Divine within them. Perhaps the Great Mother, the One who is All and Nothing, decided that diversity was good, for when I woke there was only the Void. The First Ones shaped the worlds. And there are others out there, far beyond the stars.*

"How do you know?" Manny asked. The young Healer's voice was quiet. He had come to stand by Kalla, trading intimidation for curiosity.

I am there also. I am everywhere, as is the Great Mother. Here I am Araun, but that is only a small fraction of 'who' or 'what' I really am. A tiny shard of personality, in a much greater being.

"I think my head hurts..." Aleister groaned. "This is too much to understand all at once, especially for one who only recently had it forcibly beaten into them that it is possible to live and remember many lives."

The bird on his shoulder squawked an agreement.

As they awaited the wolves' return, conversation turned to the realm of Xibalba itself. Having gotten over any initial fear, Manny, and Amaterasu alike, were bursting with questions. Kalla smiled as she watched Araun. The Lord of Xibalba was relaxed, taking great pleasure in indulging their curiosity and Kalla knew she had done well to visit. After a while the wolves returned and the group made their farewells.

Peace be with you, Lady Amaraaq. Return whenever you wish.

"Peace be with you, Lord Araun. I'll be sure do so." she said. As she had in Arkaddia, Kalla approached the Master of Xibalba and slipped her arms around his neck. She was surprised at how warm he felt. The spectral form looked as if it should have felt cold. Araun leaned against her, returning the affection. A deep, happy rumble bubbled up from his chest

They stepped back onto the spiral and the world shifted around them. As soon as they were back at their campsite, Kasai and Vander shifted.

"Thank you, Dashkele," Vander said softly. The War Mage looked thoughtful, but cheered by the meeting with his father.

Yes, thank you for inviting us. I learned much. Amaterasu said.

"*Yes, I'd certainly say we all learned a great deal,*" Aleister murmured.

Kalla chuckled, a broad smile creasing her face as she erased the great spiral.

Into the Serpent's Mouth

The ships made Port Dubrathi in good time and refueled, taking on new supplies. From there they had swung out over the Tezac, skirting the coast. Given the instructions that the Hounds had imparted, Kalla guessed that the serpent's mouth was the Ruz River, which emptied into the ocean from the Talysh Mountains. More specifically, it emptied into the ocean from between the peaks of Aganna and Fangul.

"There we are," Aleister said. Before them, the mouth of the Ruz opened out into the Tezac. Fog and low clouds obscured the mountain peaks. The Fox angled the ship and headed into the fogbank, frowning as he checked the ship's instruments. Lights in the cabin flickered on, registering the growing darkness. Turbulence shook the *Stymphalian* and Kalla felt her magister's growing alarm as they lost altitude. There was a yelp from the crew quarters and then the clicking of claws as Vander slunk up to the front. The wolf's ears were flat. He pressed against her leg and Kalla reached down, placing a comforting hand on his head. Aleister grew more alarmed a moment later, when the instruments went haywire.

"I'm flying blind here!" he said in a tight voice. He switched the controls to fully manual and struggled to control the ship. Muffled static came over the radio as the *Heracles* attempted to contact them, then fell silent.

Kalla tried not to let Aleister's growing fear get to her. She had full confidence in both his abilities to fly the ship and the fact that Ganysha would let them through. She just hoped that extended to her companions flying with them. The Healer didn't think she'd be able to forgive herself if something happened to them because they had tried to follow her.

Her fears were assuaged a moment later when the *Stymphalian* broke through the clouds and into a bright snow-covered valley. Kalla let out breath she'd not realised she was holding as, to the left and above them, the *Heracles* shot through, followed by the two wyvern. Aleister reengaged the ship's computers and let out a shaky sigh of his own as he picked up the radio to contact the other ship.

"Come in, *Heracles*. How fare you?"

"*A bit shaken up, but otherwise fine. I don't care to go through that again anytime soon.*" Lukas replied. "*How are things over there?*"

"We're all fine here."

"*Glad to hear it.*"

Kalla chuckled as she watched the *Heracles* take up a position slightly behind the *Stymphalian*. Amaterasu settled into place beside the ship, giving Kalla a wink when the mage looked out the window at her. Thiassi looped around the ships, seeming exultant at the sight of the snow. The fire wyrm gave him a tolerant look which caused Kalla to laugh.

Small specks dotted the valley floor below and when Aleister took the ship lower they resolved themselves into the shapes of shaggy-furred elephantine creatures. Their sheer size took her breath away. Not even the mammoth of Nu Ramerides were so big. The herd moved lazily along, cropping the long tundral grass as they went. A few looked up as the shadows of ship and wyvern passed over them before returning to their grazing.

"Look there," Aleister said.

Kalla turned her attention to where he pointed. There on the side of Fangul was a beautiful temple with soaring spires.

"That must be where we need to go."

Aleister banked the ship and made for the temple. He landed at the far edge of the temple's enormous courtyard, which could have held a whole fleet of small strike-fighters such as the *Stymphalian,* joined shortly by the *Heracles,* and the two wyvern.

A ruffled looking Kasai slipped from Thiassi's back. The frost wyvern fair shivered with contained excitement as the hawk quickly and efficiently undid the clasps to the soft, simple saddle. Kasai slapped the wyvern on the side of the neck in a playful gesture and watched as Thiassi sprang into the air and flew back towards the valley. Aleister went to help his brother and together they stored the saddle in the *Stymphalian's* hold.

It is cold here. Amaterasu grumbled in her mind. *We won't get in trouble if we hunt in the valley, will we?*

"I don't see why you would, Amaterasu. I doubt that Lord Ganysha would have let you through if there was nothing for you to eat. Just be respectful of his kin in the animal world."

Yes, Lady Kalla. The wyvern butted her head against Kalla, then sprang into the air and followed after Thiassi.

Kalla turned her attentions to the building before her. Graceful spires rose from a squat, domed center. Lesser domed towers were interspersed among the taller spires. The buildings look to have been crafted from blue granite, yet there were no seams to show where the stones sat.

Aleister returned carrying the case with the Quill of Ma'at within it. The Fox had finally convinced Kalla to leave the feather with the ship, in the secret vault hidden beneath the floor of the storage compartments. With all of the shields both magi placed on the ship regularly, it was well protected. Kalla's accepted the case, settling it over her shoulders.

The group crossed the courtyard and went up the steps to the broad crystalline doors. To either side immense statues rose, a matched pair of the elephantine creatures poised on their hind legs, with the world curled in their trunks. The tips of their long, curving tusks interlocked one another above the entry-way. Kalla raised her staff to tap against the door, but it swung open before she could do anything.

Enter and be welcome, Lady Amaraaq. Enter and be welcome, those who bravely travel with the Wolf that Sleeps.

Kalla gently edged through the door, the other trailing behind her like baby geese. The inner chamber was much warmer. Here vines crept flourished, forming a leafy net across floor and walls. Other plants grew out from the floor, plants such as Kalla had never seen and which quickly attracted Manny's fascination. The young Healer's secondary skills lay in Earth Wardenship, those who could work with the living earth.

A small path cut through the leafbed and Kalla followed it to the room's exit. Passing through the door, she found herself in an even larger atrium, this one mostly blanketed in soft grasses. An amber skylight cast golden shards about the room.

In the far corner of the room sat a being hunched over a small desk. Slightly taller than the average man, he was considerably heavier than any mere human. Thin red fur covered his body, so far as they could see. Large ears tufted in a light red fanned the air for a moment, then a slender trunk rose up to reach for something on a shelf above where he worked.

Kalla stepped closer and the being stood to face her and there was no doubt that this was Ganysha, the Elephant Lord. Ivory tusks jutted from his mouth, slightly curling inwards. His trunk coiled into a thoughtful gesture and he gave the Healer a warm smile and a slight bow of his head. Kalla returned the gestured, well aware of the fact that the others had sank to their knees and now knelt before the deity.

One is All.

"All is One," Kalla responded with a smile. They completed the greeting quickly. So often had she used it thus far that it had become a rote memorization ritual.

You may rise, fellow travelers. Ganysha looked to Kalla. *You have brought the Quill, yes?*

Kalla nodded, slipping the case from her back and presenting it to the Elephant Lord. Ganysha opened the case and reverently drew out the long white Quill.

"Can you recreate the binding parchment, Lord Ganysha?" Kalla asked.

Oh, I can. I can. But will that do any good, I do wonder. No, no. You need something more powerful. A spell of destruction rather than imprisonment. That I can do as well. That I can do, but it will take a few days of proper planning. Please make yourselves at home here in our realm. Ganysha said, then added almost as an afterthought. *Worry not about the wyvern hunting. The herds need to be kept on their toes and there are only the sluggish snow wurms to hunt them.*

"Thank you for the offer, my Lord. Tell me, is there anything you wish me to do for you while I am here?" Kalla asked.

Ah, you wish to know how to free us, yes? For that you must speak to my Lady Laeksheen. If you go through the right hand door and take the next two lefts you will find her. My Lady can also provide you with rooms and food, should you so wish.

Kalla bowed and thanked Ganysha, though the deity had already turned his attentions back to the scribe's table, tapping the Quill against his trunk.

* * *

Kalla and her companions followed Ganysha's instructions and found themselves in another vine-wrapped room. A small brook ran through this one, passing through arched recesses in the walls. Across the way a lady tended a small bed of flowers. She rose as they entered. The lady was tall and willowy, with the looks of an Ishkaran. Kalla bowed and exchanged the proper greeting to Laeksheen. When she was finished, she repeated her request to the Lady.

Welcome, Lady Amaraaq. Welcome, travelers. Come, follow me. I will take you to where you may rest and I will tell you what you need to know.

The group obediently followed Laeksheen through the Temple complex. As with the other rooms, each new one they passed through was a wonder to behold; a veritable treasure of plant-life from the world 'round and from ages past. They ended up in a small rounded terminus with a series of small chambers branching from it. The rooms looked out onto the valley below and Kalla could see the faint specks of the two hunting wyvern.

The Healer turned to find Laeksheen behind her. The Lady tapped the surprised mage on the forehead. Kalla's face went slack as hauntingly beautiful *sarisrima* music filled her mind. Laeksheen handed her a wrapped bundle, which proved to contain one of the delicate instruments.

And now you know how to free us, though you will not be able to do so until you leave our realm. I would ask that you go to the nearest temple so that the Priests may hear you play and remember the Song.

Kalla bowed. "I thank you, Lady Laeksheen. I will do so as soon as I am able."

Laeksheen left them to their own devices, telling them to wander freely through the Temple. If they wished anything, they merely had to ask it and it would appear in their rooms. They passed the rest of the day exploring the many rooms with all their exotic plant life. As evening approached they returned to their own quarters and ate.

The next few days passed in utter contentment. Laeksheen spent time with them, patiently answering the questions that Kalla and Manny peppered her with in regards to the flora. Vander disappeared several times for hours on end. Kasai as well, though they discovered that the hawk had often been out flying with Thiassi. A few times Kalla had gone out with him, to fly with Amaterasu.

During one such excursion Kalla had the fortune to see a hunting polar wurm. She and Amaterasu had been perched on a craggy cliff-face watching the herds below when the snow-covered ground seemed to *roll*, rippling out in waves. The herd panicked and stampeded as a giant, tripartite maw shot from the turf, snaring a helpless beast and swallowing it whole. The wurm's head swayed lazily, a forked tongue occasionally flickering out.

The polar wurms were far distant kin to the wyvern. Massive creatures that lived solely underground, they had thick, horny muzzles whose lower parts were split in twain. Stubby spikes adorned the polar wurm's muzzle, helping it to burrow through the frozen landscape. Thick scales armored the long, limbless body. Being subterranean dwellers, wurms lacked eyes. Instead, their muzzles were pitted with pockmarks called heat-pits. Those and the flickering tongues helped the wurms to find food, though they did not often have to seek it. Wurms could go weeks between meals.

While most dragon-kin were relegated to the continent of Su Ramerides, wurms were found on Inkanata and Ne Ramerides. The desert wurms were smaller than the polar ones, with finer scales and no spikes about the muzzle. Kalla had heard stories of great oceanic wurms far bigger than even the polar wurms.

Satisfied that there was no other food nearby, the wurm slowly disappeared back into the earth from whence it had come, leaving a great gaping hole that filled itself back in as the wurm moved beneath the surface. Kalla and Amaterasu took off from their perch a short time later and returned to the temple. The wyvern dropped the mage off and departed once more, heading back to the crags for the night.

Lady Amaraaq, will you please join me in the main Hall? Ganysha's soft voice sounded in her mind. Kalla made her way back to the Elephant Lord's Hall. She approached and gave him a small bow, which he returned. His ears fanned the air as he regarded her for a long moment, then his trunk uncoiled and dropped a bound scroll into her hands. Delicate script filled the thick parchment. Kalla ran her fingers along the edges, before looking to Ganysha.

"This will destroy Al'dhumarna? For good this time?" she asked.

That it will. That it will. Ganysha sighed. *Though it pains me to do such a thing. It is hardly the Nagali's fault that he was created thus. Yet he will destroy all if he is not stopped.* The Elephant Lord handed her a slender case and she slipped the scroll into it, stashing it within the hidden compartments of her robes.

You must seek Grael's Fang next. That weapon is the only one capable of piercing the Nagali's scales. Laeksheen and I have tried to descry the spear's whereabouts, but have been unable to do so. Last we knew, it was held in the lands of the dragon, far to the west of here.

Kalla nodded. She, too, had tried to seek the spear and likewise been unable to sense it at all nor glean any hint of where it might be. All she had to go on was the last known location. Perhaps the dragons would know where it was if it was not still with them.

"Thank you, Lord Ganysha. Thank you for forging the scroll and for your hospitality these past few days."

You are quite welcome, Lady Amaraaq. Quite welcome. It has been a joy and a pleasure to have you all here.

A rustling and a soft chuckle told her that the Fox had found her. She turned to favor him with a smile.

"*The scroll is finished then, milady?*" he asked.

"*It is,*" she replied. "Lord Ganysha, may we have your leave to depart tomorrow."

That you may, milady. That you may. You should make your repast now and sleep while you can.

She and Aleister made their way back to the rooms they shared with the others. They found Vander's door well-shut and warded. A grumpy Kasai shared a meal with the others and they called Kalla and Aleister to join them.

"What is he doing, locked away in there?" Kalla asked. Kasai scowled at her.

"I have no idea. His mind is closed to me, save for the fact that he is well enough."

"You worry too much, brother. One might think you a watchful mother hawk whose chick has gone astray," Aleister said with a grin. Kasai turned the scowl on him, eyes narrowed dangerously.

"Yes, Kasai. You shouldn't worry so, though I am thankful that you do. Vander's last magister was not nearly so attentive," Kalla said softly.

The hawk's face relaxed a bit. Vander had shared little of his experiences with Shingar, but what he had shared had given Kasai an insight into why the Dashmari acted as he did at times.

As if their conversation had lured him outside, Vander opened the door and stepped out carrying something cupped in his hands. The War Mage wore a pair of thin-lensed glasses that gave him a dignified appearance. He seemed somewhat confused to see them all clustered in the cul-de-sac, but his face lit up when his eyes found Kalla. He walked over to the Healer and held out his closed hands. Giving him a puzzled look she held out her hand and the War Mage carefully placed something in it.

Kalla stared at the small red bundle, then gasped as it shuddered and unfurled itself to reveal a tiny clockwork dragon. The little creature was exquisitely detailed with tiny overlapping scales of an iridescent ruby color. Minuscule gears whirred as the dragon stretched its wings and walked to the edge of her palm, where it sat staring up at her with a quizzical expression. Kalla understood the glasses now, as well as why Vander had remained closeted away. Artisans and Artificers wore them to aid in their work. Now that she was paying attention she saw the loupe, an instrument for even more precise work, hanging from a cord around his neck.

"For you, Lady Amaraaq," he said softly.

"It's beautiful, Vander. Thank you. But where did you get the materials for such a creation, much less the tools for it?" Kalla replied.

"Justina gave me her tools before we left Argoth. She said she had more at home and I would get better use out of these. As for the materials, I asked the Lady Laeksheen for them."

"Vander, this work, it would put a Master Artisan and a Master Artificer both to shame. When we return home, you will have little trouble passing the tests to qualify as a maester in those areas. Hauss' tests too, for that matter"

"I am glad you like it, Dashkele."

"I do," she replied. "Now come, join us for dinner."

"Yes, please do. Else the mother hen's feathers will get even more ruffled," Aleister said with a sly grin.

Vander turned puzzled eyes to Aleister, completely missing the murderous look Kasai was giving the Fox. The hawk's glare promised revenge at the first convenient moment. Manny laughed into his drink as Kalla lifted a hand to her shoulder. The tiny dragon climbed onto it and curled up.

"We leave in the morning. Lord Ganysha has finished the scroll. Our next task is to find Grael's Fang. The last known location was in Su Ramerides. I would however, like to visit Persiali,

Zhōnggu, Nihon and the Maracca before we leave this region. I would be remiss if I did not make the offer to free the Patrons of those lands as well," Kalla said.

"But what of us, Lady Kalla? Can we... can Lukas and I continue to travel with you?" Manny asked. The younger Healer bit his lip, offering her a shy smile.

"I see no reason why not. If he is willing, you can continue training with Vander."

"Of course, Dashkele. I have no problems with that," Vander said.

Manny let out a long breath. "Oh, thank you!"

"Come now. You didn't really think we would just turn you away, did you?"

"I was afraid you might consider our presence a burden, Lady Kalla."

"No burden, not at all. Merely in need of asserting your own authority. You will learn that too, no doubt. You are young, but you are still a maester of the Kanlon. Traveling with us will certainly help you learn that," Kalla replied.

"Yes, it will help. You seem afraid that others won't take you seriously, but they will as long as you don't show them your uncertainty. You do act a frightened cub sometimes, pup," Vander said. He softened his voice. "Rule number one of the War Mage's code is what?"

"It is... to face your fears," Manny said.

"And rule two?" Vander asked.

"It is to... ensure that your enemies never discover your fears."

"Just so. Keep your fears hidden from others. You are afraid of dealing with royalty. Hide that fear and treat them with respect, but not obeisance. You are magi and magi are above any and all royalty," Vander growled.

"Yes, Lord Vander, I will try act accordingly," Manny said.

"Keep your fears hidden from others, but learn to dance with them," Kasai said. "Embrace your fears, confront them, and eventually they will no longer be your fears. What you were once afraid of might even seem laughable."

"What do you fear, Master Kasai?" Manny asked. The hawk gave the young mage a long look before answering.

"I fear magick," he replied. "I fear magick, yet I've had no choice but to learn to deal with it. It doesn't seem quite so terrible anymore."

Grael's Fang

Port Auschain, Ishkar, Inkanata, Year of the Mythril Serpent, 2014 CE

After leaving Ganysha's realm, Kalla had taken the *sarisrima* to the nearest temple and played the Song for the priests there. There had been visits to the various countries of Inkanata, where Kalla and Aleister would visit the Patrons of the land through dream journeys and follow the instructions of each.

Once they reached the Marraca, Kalla turned her attention to the land itself. The oases had dried up, leaving an already parched land bereft of what little water it had. Under the Healer's influence the waters returned, restoring the deserts to the still dangerous, yet not so treacherous, shifting sands they had always been.

From there, they made the long trek to Su Ramerides. Kalla met the Patrons, and healed the land before turning attention to their next goal- tracking down Grael's Fang. Much of Su Ramerides was devoid of human habitation. It was a land of dense tropic jungle and sweeping volcanic vistas. It was among the deep jungle and high mountains that they would find the reclusive dragon clans.

Kalla stared out the window, watching the endless canopy of jungle pass beneath the *Stymphalian*. Before them loomed the great volcanic mountains, some still steaming gently. Below them, she saw Amaterasu and Thiassi swooping playfully around one another. Kasai and the War Mage were tiny specks upon their backs.

The strident blare of the *Stymphalian's* proximity sensors tore the Healer from her reverie. A shadow fell over the ship and something thudded hard against the roof.

"What in the blue hell," Aleister swore. He hissed out a sharp breath as the immense shape of a dragon eclipsed their view. The wyvern had been terrifying enough, but this beast dwarfed the *Stymphalian* and *Heracles* both. Aleister hurriedly activated the ship's shields, while Kalla wove her own around the ship.

The behemoth dove in front of them, roaring a challenge that rattled the tiny ship. Gunmetal grey scales glinted in the sunlight. Unlike the smaller wyvern that now circled it, roaring their own challenges, the dragon had four paws. Unfathomably broad wings fanned the air, throwing the ship into shadow.

A series of spikes ran down along the creature's back, terminating at the tail's tip in a deadly flail. Stubby spikes lined a slender jaw, and two larger spikes jutted from the corners of the leviathan's muzzle. The dragon roared again and swatted at the wyvern that continued to circle it, spitting fire and ice. From his place on Amaterasu's back, Vander also assaulted the dragon with fire and lightning. The *Heracles* joined the fray, ion cannons firing in rapid succession.

The ion blasts scored direct hits, washing over the dragon. Sparks of electricity danced along its spikes and the great chest swelled. The dragon opened its jaws and more electricity danced between the muzzle spurs. It roared again, spitting lightning at its tiny assailant.

The *Heracles* darted away, scarce avoiding the blast. They continued to circle the dragon, though they fired no more shots. The lesson had been learned.

The behemoth's head twisted, keeping an eye on all four as it continued to hover in the air. Sparks danced along the spikes in preparation of another attack. Amaterasu, flying above the dragon, suddenly darted towards the beast's head.

Kalla inhaled sharply, breath catching in her throat, as a tiny figure tumbled from the wyvern. Snapping jaws barely missed Amaterasu as she backwinged away from the dragon. The Healer let out a shaky breath at seeing Vander land solidly on the dragon's neck, ending up between two of the deadly spikes.

An almost comical look of surprise crossed the creature's face, then it turned and fled from them, speeding away in the direction they had been headed. The wyvern shot off after the dragon, Aleister and Lukas following behind. Kalla fretted, worried for the War Mage's safety. A smile ghosted across her face, imagining the scolding Kasai was giving his charge at the moment.

The dragon slowed as it approached the Astavi mountain range. As it did, two more colossal dragons rose from the dense jungle foliage to challenge it. They hung in the air, twin jewels illuminated by a setting sun. Unlike the first, these dragons were more colorful, one emerald-scaled, the other golden. The pair flanked the grey dragon and all three headed for an extinct volcano. The top of the mountain had been blown off long ago, and in the crater left behind, the blue waters of a lake glittered. Mists swirled in the caldera, obscuring, then revealing an island hidden at the lake's center.

The dragons descended to the island, with the wyvern and ships close behind. They landed in a clearing and moved back, craning slender necks to watch the ships land, but offering no violence. The grey dragon reached up and plucked Vander from his place on its neck. Kasai shifted form and fluttered to the War Mage's shoulder, promptly biting his ear.

"Ow! Punch a hole next time. At least then I can wear an earring…" Vander muttered. The harrier made a noise as if to say, *I can do that.* Vander reached up and clamped a hand around the bird's beak as he started to snap at the ear again. Kalla stifled a laugh at Kasai's muffled noise of irritation.

"Lady Kalla, may I introduce Chac. I've told her what we are seeking and why. I don't think you are going to like her news though," Vander said.

"I greet you, Lady of Wolves, and welcome you to our lands. The two with me are Xemenek and Ramac," Chac said. At her words, the emerald and golden dragons inclined their heads to the Mage.

"I would say that I am sorry for having attacked you, but of late we have had too many intruders, human and otherwise, who mean us nothing but harm. But is it true, what your brave companion has told me? That you are the one who restored our lands?" the grey dragon continued.

"It is true, Lady Chac," Kalla replied. "I have healed the lands and I intend to put an end to the cause. I promise you, we mean you no harm. We come seeking the artifact known as Grael's Fang. With it we hope to end Al'dhumarn's threat once and for all."

The dragons hissed at the mention of the Nagali. Chac lowered her muzzle to Kalla's level, giving the mage a greater appreciation for just how *big* the dragons were. If Chac had been so inclined, Kalla would have been no more than an appetizer for the giant creature.

"I am sorry, Lady of Wolves, but the spear is no longer in our care," Chac replied.

"What happened to it?" Kalla asked.

"The Reaversssss came and ssstole it from uss. They came in the night and they took what was most preciousss to uss. They broke our eggss and ssstole the sspear and the Eye. They sslaughtered our young and there are sso few of us left," Xemenak hissed. Her wings flared out in agitation, and she clawed the ground, rending great furrows in the loamy soil.

"The Reavers killed most of the Guardians as well," Ramac rumbled. Trees shook as his massive tail lashed against them.

"Guardians?"

"Yess. The sspear of the Dragon Goddessss and her very Son himself are guarded by the *wyvere*. They are the Guardians of the Isle of Mistsss," Xemenak said.

He gave out an eerie barking cry. After a moment the call was answered and three strange creatures loped from the trees to join the dragons. They were unlike any creature Kalla had ever seen, yet it was clear they were dragon-kin.

The *wyvere* walked upright on powerfully muscled legs that terminated in three toes, the innermost of which sported a massive sickle-shaped claw held retracted above the others. Long arms with slender, clawed fingers were tucked against a streamlined body. Leathery wings furled tight against their sides and a stiff tail swayed behind their bodies, helping them to keep balance. The creatures lifted narrow muzzles, scenting the air as they approached.

They made bobbing bows to the dragons and the lead one came up to Kalla and Aleister. It looked them over with a predatory gaze. Up close, the *wyvere* towered over the humans.

I welcome you to our island, Lady of Wolves. I am Baksa. I lead what is left of the wyvere. Lady Xemenak has told us of why you are here. She speaks truth. The spear is gone from our care, as is the Eye of the Dragon God. We have been shamed in our duty.

"Greetings, Baksa. Tell me… what is this Eye? Another artifact of some kind?"

No, Lady, not truly. It is the eye of Orius himself. Baksa replied. *Come, we will take you to the Temple of the Chained One. It is not far from here.*

Chac reached out and lifted Vander, cradling the Dashmari in one massive paw, with the harrier still perched on his shoulder. Xemenak and Ramac plucked the other magi and their magisters up, cradling them likewise. They launched themselves skyward, stirring up leaves and setting the trees to swaying violently. Behind them, the wyvern and wyvere took flight.

The mists thickened the deeper they went into the island's interior. The vespertine gloom revealed ghostly shapes that resolved into the high stone walls of an ancient temple as the dragons landed. Twisted metal gates gaped open, revealing a courtyard beyond. Within, a dark shape loomed menacingly.

The dragons let them down and as Kalla moved closer, the form resolved itself into the adamantine statue of a prone dragon that dwarfed even the leviathans behind her. Thick chains bound the feet and neck to the ground. An empty eye socket glared down at the tiny mage who had the effrontery to dare approach. An orb of zarconite filled the other socket.

This is Orius, the Grey. Bahamut's twin. The Lady of Chaos bound him here, long, long ago. It was our task to watch over him and make sure nothing happened to him. The Fang, too, was kept here. Baksa said.

"Why was Orius bound here?" Manny asked. The young mage moved up beside Kalla and placed a hand on one of the massive claws.

"Listen then, young one and I will tell you," Ramac rumbled. "Then you will understand just how terrible a thing it is that the Eye is gone.

"Long ago, when the world was young, the Lord of Death grew disillusioned with the creations of his forebears. Of a mind to recreate the world the great Grey Dragon wrought a holocaust of death upon all life. Pestilence and plague swept the lands, taking life before it was due.

"The air grew colder, the waters freezing into great sheets of blue-grey ice. Plants and trees perished, as did the fish of the sea and the birds of the air. Famine and starvation turned all creatures upon one another.

"When the Patrons beheld the devastation, they sent Bahamut after his twin, but the Lord of Time was unable to sway his brother from his terrible course. Orius continued his war against life, til it seemed as if the very bonds of Time itself seemed destined to collapse and return the world to the Void from which it had been Created.

"Grael, the Mother of Chaos, grew angry with her Son and stood against him, tooth and claw. The battle shook the very foundations of the earth itself, but in the end the Mother prevailed, for even Death itself cannot stand against the purity of wild, untamed Chaos.

"Grael would have sent her son to Oblivion, but Ayahz, the Father of Life, beseeched her to have mercy. So it was that Orius was bound upon the Isle of Mists, shackled by chains of stardust. After the Lord of Death was sealed away, Bahamut shouldered his brother's mantle, aided by Carron Deathbringer.

"As the aeons rolled by the great dragon's immortal body turned to adamantine as the mind brooded, slumbering fitfully, only vaguely aware of the passing ages. It may be that Orius will awaken to once again join the ranks of the Dragon Patrons, but this only the One who is All and Nothing knows. The Eye that was taken contains all the power of the Dragon God, if one could but learn to use it." Ramac finished his story and sat back on his haunches.

"Fennec Nall mentioned the Crescent Reavers. He said they called themselves the *rahksa*. What are they exactly? Is there any way we can find them?" Kalla asked.

"The Reaversss are dragon-kin, Great Lady. Warped and twisssted dragon-kin. You will not find them, ssso long asss they do not wisssh to be found," *Xemenek* hissed. "We tried. We would have reclaimed what was oursssss, but to no avail. They come and go as the wind, bringing death and destruction."

Kalla shook her head. "I am at a loss as to what to do then. We cannot continue to search blindly, yet we cannot proceed either."

"I hate to say it, but if they belong to the Nagali, then sooner or later we can assume they will come after you, milady," Aleister said. "Maybe then we will get the chance to obtain the spear or its location."

The Healer frowned, but nodded. "Perhaps. I don't like putting any of you in such danger though."

"Don't even think about it," Vander growled. "We aren't leaving you to be hunted by these things. You are safer with us than without."

The dragons carried them from the temple to caves within the caldera walls, and there the magi saw the aftermath left behind by what they sought to hunt themselves. Wounded dragons and *wyvere* filled the chambers. Strewn about were the trampled remains of earthen nests and shattered eggs. Pools of dried blood and albumen, some bearing imprints of the fallen, dotted the cavern floors, though the bodies had been removed. The three magi set to work, healing the dragons and *wyvere* who yet lived.

When Aleister finally made Kalla stop because she was starting to drain his own energy, she found that both Manny and Vander had long since ceased working and were fast asleep from their efforts, with their magisters standing a weary guard. The Fox gently guided her over to them and pushed her down beside Vander. She was asleep almost before she hit the floor, utterly drained from the work.

* * *

Ashen heat blew across the Healer's face and her eyes flew open. She was in the dream world, of that much she was certain. Dark clouds roiled in the sky, tinged a bloody red. She was standing on a bare island, amidst a sluggish sea of lava that inexorably made its way past.

Smoky laughter came from behind her and Kalla turned to face a black-scaled dragon of immense proportions, bigger than even the sleeping Orius. Ruby-red eyes glittered from beneath great curling ram-horns, peering down a slender, barbeled muzzle at the tiny mage. A mane of fur ran down the dragon's long slinky neck and tufted the ankles and elbows as well. Black feathery wings flared open as the dragon sat back on its haunches.

All is One. The dragon said in a smoky voice. Kalla's eyes widened as she realized this must be Grael the Black, the Lady of Chaos herself.

"One is All," Kalla responded.

As above.

"So below."

"*Thus are all Connected.*"

Greetings, Lady Amaraaq. Thank you for healing the lands of my children. You came here seeking my Fang. Though it be stolen, I will give you what you need to forge another. You have a talented Artificer and Artisan traveling with you. The Lady Laeksheen has given him the materials to craft such a weapon. I will give you what you lack.

The black dragon opened her jaws wide, reaching far into her mouth. With a sudden *tug* she withdrew her paw. In her claws Grael held a foot-long serrated tooth which she gently passed off to Kalla.

Careful now. It is sharp.

"Thank you, Lady Grael. We will make good use of your gift."

That is my hope, Empress of Wolves. That is my hope. We would also like to ask if you would free us as you have freed the others of our 'family'.

"Family?" Kalla asked.

You think of the Patrons of the various lands as all one rather bizarre family, little Wolf. That we are- one big family.

"I would be honored to do so, Lady Grael," the mage said. She looked down at the fang in her hands, then back up at the leviathan looming above her. "Lady Grael, is it true? Are you and yours as old as Araun?"

A snort came from further behind the black dragon. The air shimmered, then coalesced into first one, then another, then another towering dragon. In the end, seven dragons stood ranged about her, as different from one another as they could be.

A pearly-scaled dragon dipped its head to her. This dragon looked much like Grael in his body form, the only difference being that he had leathery wings instead of feathered ones. Bright blue eyes regarded her with loving patience. Kalla guessed that it was Ayahz, Grael's mate.

We are nearly as old as Father Araun. We were among the first created from the One.

"How did you survive the years when so many others did not?" Kalla asked.

Our children have longer memories and longer lives. They are not as fickle as the younger, short-lived races. This from a stocky, blunt-muzzled dragon scaled in silver-grey. Thick horns jutted back from his heavy brow and he unfurled leathery wings, fanning the air gently. This would be Bahamut then, Kalla thought. Orius' brother.

That is not the point now is it? A red dragon said testily, fixing a fierce orange gaze on the group. He looked like Bahamut, save for his scales shone like trapped firelight and jet black horns adorned his head.

Do not be silly, Freyeth. The new one come among us is welcome to learn. She is part of the family now. An emerald green dragon chided Freyeth in gentle feminine tones and he withdrew with a slightly abashed look. The green dragon, Lady Gaia, was long and slinky, lacking wings. Stubby horns framed her head.

Please excuse my mate, Lady Amaraaq. He speaks truth though. Will you free us?

"Certainly, I will do as I may, if only you will tell me how," Kalla said. "Only, I thought that I had freed the Patrons of Su Ramerides."

You freed the Patrons of this land. We, however, hold sway over a land far from these shores. We are present here because here it is that the dragons dwell.

No fancy Song do we have for you, but a great artifact most certainly. An odd serpentine dragon covered in blue-grey feathery scales came forward. This dragon, Rai, looked like the wyvern, with two wings and two feet, though his wings were feathery. A great feathered crest framed his crocodalian head and it was in those massive jaws that he held an object. Gently he lowered his head to Kalla's level and let her withdraw a large hunting horn. The Healer gasped at its beauty, for it was covered with scales of myriad colors. There were scales of pearly opalescence, those of iridescent obsidian, darkly shining silver, glittering carmine and shimmers of azure and emerald. The edging of the horn was decorated with wispy feather scales akin to Rai's.

You need merely blow the Horn called Dragon's Dirge to free us, as easy a task as the one Father Araun gave you. The last of the clustered dragons was the blue-scaled wurm Tiama'at. Like her earthly children, the great dragon goddess had massive tri-partite jaws. Limbless and wingless, she was coiled in a great shimmering sapphire heap.

Go now. Grael rumbled. *Go now and use the Horn when you can. Take it with you, for its haunting call can immobilize and disorient the wretched Kin, the Crescent Reavers. You will have an advantage over them they will not be expecting. And seek you out they will, once they realize that you have crafted a new spear.*

"I will do so, Great Ones," Kalla said.

And best of luck to you, with our thanks, Lady Amaraaq. Grael said as Kalla began to fade from the smoke-tinged realm of the dragons.

Sunlight streamed through the cave entrance, spilling over Kalla and warming the stones. Grumbling, the Healer grudgingly woke to find Aleister watching her with a slight grin. She groaned and shifted to find that she had been lying upon the jagged tooth. The Horn she found clutched protectively to her chest.

The Fox's smile broadened when he saw she was awake and he held out a waterskin to her. As she took it Kalla noticed that Vander and Manny still slept. Kasai and Lukas slept now as well. The wyvern were gone, most likely hunting. Aleister was busy tending a small fire over which the carcasses of two capybara sizzled tantalizingly. Kalla winced as her tummy growled.

"The dragons brought them for us. I went ahead and started cooking them, though sadly we have no spices or such. Figured you'd be hungry when you woke.

"We took it in turn to watch over you. Lucky or unlucky, I got the last watch," he said. *"The others haven't budged a bit. No matter what you might think of the role a magister plays, I can certainly see why the magi are required to have one."*

Kalla gave him a sour look and handed the waterskin back. While Aleister finished cooking breakfast, Kalla's made her rounds to check on the recovering dragons. By the time she returned, the others had woken and the capybara were finished cooking. The Fox handed her a cooled piece as she settled down beside him. Kalla took it gratefully, murmuring a soft thanks.

"How were they doing, Dashkele?" Vander asked.

"They are all doing well. You both did good work," she said.

"Did we heal all of them?" Manny looked to her hopefully.

"Aye, all of them that needed it."

"I'm glad."

Kalla nodded, then gently withdrew the long fang from within her robes. She'd dulled the edge with a shield so she wouldn't accidentally maim herself.

"The Lady Grael was gracious enough to give us a new tooth," Kalla said. "She said you would be able to craft a new spear, Vander."

Vander took the tooth from her and looked at it from all angles, sinking into the absent-minded mode that meant he was thinking of possibilities.

One of the dragons, an amethyst beauty, lumbered over to them and lowered her head to Kalla's level.

"Thank you, for healing us," the purple leviathan murmured sadly. Kalla reached out and gently placed a hand on one of the dragon's talons. The Healer knew, from her work, that this young female dragon had lost not an egg, but a dragonet in the attack.

"I know what you lost, young one. I grieve with you. If it is in our power we will repay the Reavers for your losses.

"Nay, Great Lady, do not seek them out. To meet them is to meet death itself. Our young were slaughtered mercilessly, the eggs targeted specifically.

"They were everywhere that night. No place was safe. The dragonets and the eggs, those are the greatest loss for us. They were our future, the future of the dragons and of the *wyvere*."

"I do not intend to seek them out, but I have every reason to think they will come hunting for me. If they do, we will be ready, and we will avenge you and your kin," Kalla said.

"How can you hope to stand against them when even we could not, Great Lady?"

"With this."

Kalla gathered up the Horn and went to stand at the cave's entrance. Below them spread a vast panorama encompassing the crater lake and its mist-shrouded island, as well as the canopy of jungle beyond. In the distance a volcano steamed gently. Wispy plume of smoke rose lazily into the morning sky.

Kalla raised the Horn, running her hands over the glittering scales, then put it to her lips and blew. A deep mournful sound rolled across the lake, echoing from the surrounding mountains. The echoes died away, followed by a hint of smoky laughter drifting with the breeze.

Xemenek and Ramac had come to the cave's entrance and now stood beside the Healer.

"Where did you get that?" the great gold-scaled dragon asked.

"I received it from the Seven. They said it would be useful against the Reavers," Kalla replied. "However, it is a treasure of the dragons. When my task is over, I will have it and hopefully both spears returned to you. The Eye too, if it is in my power to do so."

There was only one spear taken, Great Lady.

"Lady Grael gave me the means to have another created. My companion can do so."

Wolf's Fury

Sunset swirls of purple and rose shone through the wispy clouds. Thin streamers of smoke drifted up from the forest floor, catching Kalla's attention as the *Stymphalian* flew by.

"Aleister, turn back," she said. The Fox patiently obliged as Kalla radioed the *Heracles*. They overflew the clearing from which the smoke rose. Aleister brought the ship to ground, the *Heracles* landing nearby.

"What happened here?" the Fox asked as they surveyed the damage at a more personal range. Blackened grass and the charred remains of trees covered a near perfect circle.

"The area was warded," Vander said. "A weak ward, but enough to stop the flames." The War Mage shuddered. "And the fire was elemental fire. This was a summoner's work."

"A summoner? You don't think this is Grosso's work do you?" she asked.

"I don't know any other summoners, do you?"

Kalla called out to Jahnsen, hoping the flame elemental could shed some light on what happened. Smoke coalesced and coiled about her as the elemental responded to her call and she put her question to him.

Indeed, Great Lady. There were elementalsss here, not sssso long ago. Jahnsen uncoiled from Kalla and darted around the ruined clearing, his smoky form flashing from place to place. When he was done, Jahnsen returned to the Healer's side.

Two flame elementalss and an earth elemental, Great Lady. Sssomething elsse here, too. Sssomething dangerous. This was a ssslaver'sss camp. Jahnsen hissed. *The slaves made it out before the camp was desstroyed, but the ssslaverss did not. They died here.*

Kalla walked through the area, concentrating. Now that she knew what to look for, it was easy to sense the deaths that had taken place here. Sifting through the ashes, Kalla shivered as she touched fragments of bone. Each shard, each tiny touch, passed fading memories to her.

The slavers' deaths had been as unpleasant as the men themselves, brutal, harsh, and unforgiving. Images of their final moments flashed through her mind. Screams, panic, half-seen glimpses of *something* that looked to be covered in a thin black fur or feathers and moved like the wind itself. The smoky voice of Tama and a rumbling growl like that of rocks in a landslide.

"Tama was here, and that means Grosso was too. Why would he have let the slaves go? Why would he care in the first place?" Kalla murmured.

"I cannot say, Dashkele," the War Mage said. "This is a cursed place. We should leave."

Though Rinsook was close, Kalla wanted to contact the Patrons of Rang'moori out away from a village or town. Dinner was done and the sun had long since sunk beyond the horizon, going to its nightly slumber. The moon had risen, full and bright.

Kalla was resting against Amaterasu's side, reading. Vander lay next to her, in his wolf form. Closer to the campfire Manny and the magisters sat huddled around a pair of *chigali* boards.

A panicked cry of a distressed child split the night. Vander jumped up, ears pricked forward and mane fluffed. A deep bass growling filled the wolf's chest and he suddenly darted from the clearing, passing through the wards. Both Arkaddians followed him into the darkness beyond as the child cried out again. A man's scream came next, cut off rather abruptly.

"*Aleister? Are you okay? What's going on?*" Kalla asked, sharing a look with Manny. By the fire, the younger Healer's eyes were wide with fear and uncertainty.

"*A slaver, milady. Chasing a young boy. Vander has... taken care of the man. We are returning now,*" the Fox said.

It wasn't long before the three returned, Aleister carrying a young boy. The child, barely five years old, had a dull listless look in his eyes as if resigned to whatever fate they had in store for him.

Kalla frowned and took the child from her Aleister, murmuring soft words of comfort. It took the boy a moment to focus on her, but when he did tears filled his blue eyes and he buried his head against her, sobbing.

The Healer gently rocked him, making soft shushing noises. She allowed her gift to flow through him, easing his evident fear and distress and in doing so found the cause. Kalla grew sick at heart with what had been done to the child. Without looking up she spoke to the three that had brought him in.

"There are more out there, if you follow the boy's trail back. Find them and when you do, show them no mercy," she said in a flat voice. Vander turned without a word and trotted back into the darkness with the two Arkaddians shadowing him in silence.

* * *

The wolf bent his head to his task, following the child's scent trail. Behind him, Aleister and Kasai moved silently through the forest. By this time all three knew what Kalla had learned and each was just as angry as the Healer.

The clearing they came to was small. This wasn't a full slaver's camp like the other had been. These men had been out hunting and were now making their way back home.

Safe in the shadowed forest, Vander shielded the magisters, then melted back into the shadows. Like a wraith the wolf circled the small camp, laying wardings of containment as he went. From within the camp he heard the sound of soft sobbing and once a pleading female voice that quickened his pace in anger. It was hard to see into the camp, as far back in the woods as he was, but the War Mage counted three tents. A fire blazed in the middle with a lone man attending it.

Rejoining the magisters, Vander shifted and wordlessly gestured for them to circle the camp in opposite directions. He waited until he heard Kasai's whistling nightbird cry float through the trees, followed by Aleister's response, then plunged into the clearing, igniting the wards behind him. The man at the fire jumped up in alarm and fell back again just as suddenly, a dagger buried in his throat.

Using his magick, Vander uprooted the first tent, and flung it aside, only to find the source of the pleading voice. The War Mage roared in wordless fury, ripping the slaver off of his victim, his anger doubled by the fact that the slaver was Dashmari. The man was dead before he hit the ground.

Vandet snarled, ears flat, as two more men fled from the tent, while the terrified young woman tried desperately to gather the blankets about herself. Another Dashmari, a brother by scent, stayed to fight, but he fared no better than the first.

Vander turned and sent something spinning after the two runners. The objects sparked with lightning as they spun through the air, growing larger as they went. The spinning disks struck the men, decapitating one and severing the arm of the other.

A dagger buried itself in the fallen man's chest, silencing his agonized cries as the disks came back to the War Mage. He caught them easily and spun them on his fingertips as more men poured from one of the larger remaining tents.

Vander launched them again, cutting down two more men, taking out a third with a bolt of brilliant purple lightning. Dismayed cries rang through the camp as the slavers realized that they were trapped with the enraged War Mage and the magisters.

Vander stood amidst the wreakage of the camp, panting heavily. He shrank the artifice disks and tucked them away before turning his attention back to the young woman. Honey-blond hair spilled down around her tear-streaked face as she stared up at him. The Rang'moori woman whimpered as she tried to pull the blankets tighter around herself.

"Please don't hurt me," she whispered.

Vander knelt before her. Beneath the young woman's fear laced scent of sun-ripened blackberries, the War Mage caught the scent of honeysuckle.

"Don't worry. We're here to help you," he said softly. She flinched and cringed back from him.

"Emmeline! Leave her alone!"

Vander spun just in time to see a Sveltlander woman swinging a heavy sword at him. He caught her easily in coils of air and gently took the sword away as Kasai came running up.

"I have no intention of hurting her," the War Mage said. He released the Sveltlander warily and she darted to Emmeline's side, giving Vander and Kasai an angry look. Aleister shepherded the remaining slaves over to them. They were a motley group of children and women, each wearing a braided slave collar. The collection scent of resignation caught in Vander's throat, and he struggled not to gag. Ranni chased the War Mage and magisters away, and helped Emmeline to dress.

Before they left, Vander razed the camp with his own brand of fire, eradicating all evidence that it had ever existed. Both Kasai and Aleister carried one of the young children. Behind them,

Emmeline struggled to keep pace. Despite Ranni's urging, the Rang'moori woman's strength was failing, depleted by fear and sheer exhaustion. Vander finally turned back, offering to carry her. She cringed away from him at first, but Ranni managed to coax her into accepting the offer. He gently scooped her up. The young woman stayed tense in his arms for a moment, then finally relaxed. She was fast asleep before they reached camp.

* * *

Kalla was waiting for them, blankets and warm food ready. The magi gave what healing they could offer. By the time they were finished, the Healer were thoroughly sick at heart. Not for the first time, Kalla cursed the fact that a Healer picked up a patient's memories. Their bodies may have been healed, but their minds were a different story. Nothing would make the things they had been subjected to any better.

"Thank you for rescuing us and feeding us. It's been a long time since we had any decent food," said one women said. There was a long moment of silence.

"What is going to happen to us now?" another asked.

"You're welcome. I regret we didn't find you sooner. We will do our utmost to return you to your families tomorrow."

"I don't have anywhere to return to," Emmeline said in a small voice. The young Rang'moori was huddled by Ranni and the Sveltlander leaned over to comfort her. Kalla caught Vander's eye and he shook his head once. A few seconds later came the soft whistling of Kasai, who was at present somewhere beyond the *Heracles* with the wyvern. The great wyrms had graciously vacated the area immediately around the ships in deference to the fearful ex-slaves. A moment after that and Aleister spoke to her.

"*Both lost their homes when taken. Emmeline lived alone, as an herbalist to a small village. Vander says she knows her stuff.*

Unfortunately, her home was burnt to the ground. She is scared to return. Ranni, on the other hand, lost a family. Her liya *and her child were killed in the raid that took her."*

Kalla nodded a slight acknowledgment. She had healed the two children. Their fragmented, childish memories had given her enough to know where to take them and if she understood correctly they had families still living who would be desperately searching for them. She had also healed two of the women, Alyssin and Willow. It had been Willow who had spoken earlier.

"If you have no place to return to, you may go to the Kanlon. They will provide a place for you, if you do not mind working for the magi. You would have a warm place to stay, never have to worry about food, and you would be paid decent wages. The offer is open to any of you who wish it," Kalla said.

"They wouldn't want us... we are tainted now...," Emmeline sobbed.

"Emmeline, look at me please," Kalla said. Emmeline glanced up briefly, then lowered her gaze back to the ground.

"No one at the Kanlon is going to think you tainted because of what you've been through. No one is going to shun you for it. It would be only the Chief Healer and the Sin' who need know exactly what had brought you there to begin with and I can promise you they will not tell anyone."

"Listen to the Lady Mage, Emmy. I'll go with you. Nothing left for me in the Sveltlands after all," Ranni said.

"Really?" Emmeline sniffled, struggling to hold back more sobs.

"Really," Vander said softly. "Lady Kalla speaks the truth. The magi will not turn you away. But you should sleep now. Tomorrow is time enough for those decisions."

"How could anyone do such a thing to another?" Vander murmured. The six sat off from the group of sleeping women and children.

"I thought what I'd been through was bad. If the work back at the clearing *was* Grosso's, I would have to thank him for that at least."

"I won't pretend to understand the workings of such depraved minds," Kalla said.

* * *

The scent of wintergrass and Kalla woke to find herself in a rolling golden field that spread as far as the eye could see.

"Now this looks familiar," Aleister said from beside her. "Please tell me the Patrons of Rang'moori don't have a penchant for windstorms..."

There was musical laughter from behind them. *No windstorms today, Prince.*

Turning, they found themselves facing three women more beautiful than Kalla had ever seen. Though each looked young, all looked wise beyond their years.

All is One. This from a lady dressed in a flowing gown of pearly white. Long brown hair threaded with hints of red framed a pair of doe-like brown eyes.

"One is All," Kalla replied.

As above. A lady with the fiery red hair of the Crannogmar-chogi spoke next. She wore a dress of dark emerald and green eyes glimmered with mirth as she greeted them.

"So below."

"*Thus are all Connected.*"

Welcome, Lady Amaraaq. Welcome, Prince Kaze. The third lady wore a dress of palest blue that matched her eyes. Her red-gold hair was plaited in many thin, long braids.

"Thank you, Great Lady," Kalla said. "You are Lady Dana?"

Indeed I am, Lady Dana replied. *I am glad you have chosen to aid us, Lady Amaraaq. These are my sisters, the Lady Dôn, of Kymru and the Lady Birgit, of the Crannongmarch.*

This is for you. The flame-haired woman stepped forward, reaching over her shoulder. She slipped a *basacaila* from her back and handed it to Kalla. As the Healer took the stringed instrument Dôn stepped forward and tapped her on the forehead. Beautiful music filled Kalla's mind- the Song that would free their lands.

I would ask something further of you, Lady Amaraaq, Dana said. *Give Hagalaz the same chance you gave your wolf. You will not regret it. And remember, young one, destruction can lead to hope. You can't have beginnings without endings, but sometimes those endings aren't as pretty as one might like.*

"I will remember the name and if I should come across them, I will do so," Kalla replied.

Oh, you will come across him, sooner or later. Remember your word, Lady Amaraaq, Dana said, her voice fading as Kalla's hold on the dream world began to slip.

The Summons

Rinsook at night was a beauty to behold, Kalla mused. The skyport was aglow with Artifice lamps, shining like fireflies about the individual paddocks. As they approached, a voice came over the radio. Aleister requested permission to land and they were directed to a paddock whose lights switched from an orange glow to a flashing blue.

The *Heracles* had yet to arrive. While the *Stymphalian* had taken the children back to their families, Lukas and Manny had taken the rescued women. Kalla and Aleister made their way back to the Jester's Balance, the inn in which they had stayed before. Though she hadn't seen the wyvern, Vander and Kasai had gone to Rinsook ahead of the others.

Ranni and Emmeline had chosen to remain with Kalla's group. The herbalist was still very quiet and withdrawn. She flinched, and drew closer to Ranni when the group entered the cheerful confines of the inn. The press of people increased her nervousness and Kalla wasted no time in acquiring a pair of rooms for the four of them.

Kalla gave quiet instructions to the innkeeper to have only female servants attend the two women and asked for food to be brought up to the rooms for all four of them. The Healer left the two women at their room with the admonition to call her if they needed anything.

"We will, Lady Mage," Ranni said. "Thank you again for helping us."

"Yes, thank you. I hope I can repay your generosity, Lady Mage," Emmeline said softly.

They disappeared into their room, and Kalla walked down to her own, where Aleister was already talking with Vander and Kasai. The War Mage and his magister had been in the dining hall when they had entered and had followed them upstairs. Vander gave her a questioning look when she entered.

"How are they?" he asked.

"They are doing as well as can be expected," Kalla replied. "Ranni is holding up better than Emmeline. The Sveltlander has the spirit and determination of her people, that's for sure. Emmeline on the other hand... well, I think it will take her longer to heal."

Vander sighed. "I know..."

The War Mage let the subject go, as a soft knocking came at the door. Aleister answered it and let in the servants bearing their dinner. After they departed the discussion turned to the Healer's trip. It had taken some work, but they had finally figured out where the children belonged. Sure enough, there were frantic families looking for them. It broke Kalla's heart to have to tell the mothers what had befallen their children, but the parents were grateful that the mage had brought them home alive.

Manny and Lukas arrived the next day, successful in returning their own charges to their families.

"We also found word of the other freed slaves. There were a few in the second village we visited and one in the last. They said that a Rang'moori mage freed them, but his House wasn't evident from his robes. They were trimmed in grey, not red. He only gave his name as 'el'Marwol'. They did say he had burn scars on his face and his right hand," Manny said.

"Well, that would be Grosso. No doubt he's figured it safer to change his name and clothes," Vander said. "That still doesn't explain *why* he helped them to begin with."

"Marwol...," Kalla muttered. "That is a Kymry word. It means 'death'. I'm not sure what 'el' means. And why grey? That's a Technomancer colour..."

"The name certainly seems to fit..." Vander muttered.

* * *

"*Kalla kyl'Solidor...*"
"*Kalla kyl'Solidor...*"
"*Kalla kyl'Solidor!*"

Kalla made an annoyed noise at the insistent voice in her head. It was too early in the morning for this. The sun hadn't even properly risen yet.

"What?!" she growled. Beside her Aleister muttered something unintelligible in Arkaddian.

"*Wake up, Lady of Wolves!*"

The Healer jolted awake at the familiar voice in her head. "Justina?"

"*None other.*"

"But then, that means you are the new 'Tem. Congratulations, Lady Justina," Kalla said. She was definitely more awake now and so was the Fox. He wrapped an arm around her and listened to her side of the conversation.

"*Many thanks, Lady Kalla. It's been a learning experience, that's for sure. But enough with the formalities. I've been asked to call you home.*

"*Never fear, both of you are welcome here. I managed to pass Hauss' test with what I learned from Vander. The Chief Healer was most pleased and the 'Sin are eager to see if you can bond more of us,"* the new Master of Solidor said.

"I'm glad to hear it," Kalla said. She filled Justina in on what they had been through since their meeting on Argoth, expressing frustration at the standstill in which they found themselves, and her anger and puzzlement regarding the slave encampments.

"I will have the Master Seer and the Chief Archivist look for any hint of the Isle of Whispers. Hopefully, we can find some answers for you.

"Ranni and Emmeline will certainly be welcome here. I will have quarters prepared and will tell Hauss and the 'Sin what you have told me. In the meantime, have a safe journey home."

"Thank you, Lady Justina. We will see you soon," Kalla replied.

"I gather we're returning to Cryshal," Aleister said.

"Didn't think it would be so soon. They want me to teach how to share gifts." Kalla's frowned. She rubbed a hand over her heart, trying to ease away the tightness building in her chest. Kalla realised she didn't want to return. There was still so much to do.

Sensing her conflict, Aleister pulled her close.

"It'll be fine, milady. It will be good for us to be there while Emmeline and Ranni get settled. We're familiar faces."

They met the others downstairs for breakfast.

"I suppose you've heard already?" Vander asked in a miserable voice as the Healer joined him. Restless energy had him fidgeting in his seat.

"Solidor has a new 'Tem. Yes, Justina contacted me as well. We have been recalled home." Kalla said.

"I don't think I am ready for this," Vander said in a pained voice. "I... I keep seeing that stone chamber, the needle... the moment when I faced you. Fought you. All I can think is that they'll still see me as a traitor. I don't want to be shunned."

Kalla reached out and placed her hand on his.

"*Don't worry. Everything will work out. You've won Lady Justina's approval. You will win Hauss' as soon as he tests you. None can say you are not a different person than you were before,*" she said.

"*Thank you for believing in me, Dashkele. Thank you for your trust,*" Vander said.

Kalla gave his hand a gentle squeeze before turning to Aleister. The Fox had been conferring with Sir Lukas, planning the course that would take them home to Cryshal Kanlon.

Cryshal Kanlon, 10000ft above the Aryth Ocean, Year of the Mythril Serpent, 2014 CE

Kalla chuckled softly at the muted gasps behind her as Ranni and Emmeline descended from their carriage and glimpsed the Kanlon up close, in all its dazzling brightness. Not that they could have missed the shining beacon on the approach to Cryshal to begin with.

A flock of strider ships had greeted them at Cryshal's boundaries and escorted them in. The swarm saw them to the paddocks and departed as quickly as it had gathered upon their arrival.

At Bensen'gar they shielded the ships and left them in the long-term hangers. Amaterasu had taken Thiassi to the forest where she had spent their last visit.

Kalla's was pleased to see that Justina had sent a carriage carrying two female Healers, their male magisters disguised as the liveried servants in charge of the carriage. The two magi had gently chivvied Ranni and Emmeline into the carriage as the rest of them climbed into the remaining one.

Now these same Healers started to hurry their charges away. Kalla frowned at the abruptness. Emmeline broke from the group, darting over and wrapping Vander in a hug. She whispered an almost silent 'thank you', and darted away again before the Dashmari could respond. Kalla chuckled as his cheeks flushed slightly in embarrassment.

Vander turned to Kalla with a slightly bemused expression, then stiffened as a group of magi exited the Kanlon; Justina, Hauss and several of the 'Sin among them. None of the magi looked happy to see them and Kalla growled softly as a grim-faced Hauss and Justina stepped up to them, flanked by two other Solidoran magi and a cluster of armed magisters.

Hauss reached out and gripped Kalla's hand in an abrupt gesture. Fear flooded her as her link to her power suddenly blinked out. She tried to pull away from the Arkaddian's strong grip, but Hauss held firm. Beside her, Kalla's heard Vander's panicked growl beside. She struggled more fiercely, fighting to get to him.

She felt Aleister's alarm, a fever-bright fear, before the connection between the two closed down. Time seemed to become suffocatingly slow, and Kalla's struggles waned. Darkness engulfed her, and the last thing she felt was Hauss' strong hands catching her as she fell.

* * *

Kalla woke slowly. Grogginess gave way to brief panic as the Healer realized her powers were still blocked, even those of Amaraaq. She was lying on a comfortable bed, so she at least wasn't in the dungeons of Cryshal. A muted glowlamp cast the small room in dim light.

The Healer's lips thinned as she sat up, surveying her surroundings. Other than the bed, and table with the glowlamp, there were no other furnishings. She paced tight circles, occasionally muttering a string of snarled profanities. Had they been lured home just so they could be fettered? Kalla wondered. And why had Hauss, of all people, been a part of such a betrayal?

Pain shot through her jaws and Kalla stopped pacing. She hadn't realised she was grinding her teeth. She had a vague sense Aleister was nearby. The link was still alive, though, like her magick, still blocked from being used.

Sorrow washed the anger away as Kalla thought of Vander, and the time he had spent with his magick bound. Granted, it had been necessary then… The Healer sank back on the bed. She wasn't sure how long she had been out, but it had been long enough that her belly grumbled unhappily for want of food.

Inspiration struck her. She called out softly for Jahnsen, but the elemental didn't come to her call and Kalla was forced to assume they couldn't hear her. Frustration gnawed at her. After a time, the Healer passed into fitful sleep.

The soft scraping of the door opening jolted Kalla out of her light doze. She growled as someone entered the room, then squinted her eyes as magelight erupted before her. Malik sin'Solidor entered, followed by his Magister. Aelfin was a thin blade of a man, Kymry, with the darker brown hair and eyes common to his people. He wore no armor, but a sword hung at his waist and Kalla knew the man was well versed in its use.

She stifled her indignation as Malik silenced her voice. He silently motioned for her to exit the room. Without waiting to see if she would follow, Malik turned and walked out. Aelfin waited, stoic and silent, until she had followed Malik out the door.

Malik lead her through a series of corridors, finally stopping before a door deep within the Kanlon, this one thick and heavy on its hinges. He turned to face her.

"When you walk through this door, your powers will be freed. You will face the new Master War Mage in the traditional test to attain maestership in War Magick. The room is well-shielded and you will not be able to communicate with your magister. May Balgeras bless you, Lady Kalla," Malik said as Aelfin pulled the door open.

Kalla glared at the older mage before stalking into the room. The Healer resisted the urge to flinch as Aelfin shut the door with a resounding clang of finality behind her.

The room was brightly lit, a vast circular space devoid of any ornamentation. As the door closed behind her, the invisible chains binding her magick fell free, though true to Malik's word, she was still unable to mind-speak Aleister.

Her opponent walked through a door on the far side of the room. As it closed behind them a ward rippled along the walls, flaring purple for an instant before disappearing. They wore the black robes of the Kanlon, trimmed in Solidor red. A hood and shroud covered their face.

Kalla frowned and drew in a deep breath. She could pick up no trace of the War Mage's scent. She put that from her mind as a streak of fire shot towards her. Her opponent had wasted no time in beginning this battle.

Kalla hastily erected a shield just before the flames engulfed her. They washed harmlessly over her instead and she sent a tentative return fire of her own as her mind raced to recall all that she had learned from Vander. Her effort was almost contemptuously batted aside, and a fresh volley of lightning twined fire was sent towards her.

Kalla strengthened her shields, tweaking them to repel attacks. Unfortunately, her opponent had the same idea and the ricochet bounced off their shield and back to Kalla. The Healer was already moving and it went past her and dissipated against the warding.

Kalla sent her magick into the ground and set the earth to trembling. A ragged furrow cut through the rock, heading for the War Mage. As it neared him, it erupted into a geyser of earthen fury. The shrouded Mage strengthened their shields and bulled through the falling stones, sending more fire and lightning her way.

Kalla frowned, tweaking her shields to absorb and contain energy. Her gamble worked and the energy washed over her, strengthening the shields. Something bright whipped by her head. As it returned to her opponent, she saw that it was a whirling disk, sparking with lightning.

She snarled as the mage gave a growling laugh, spinning a pair of disks on their fingertips. The laugh sounded masculine. He sent both disks towards her, fire and lightning dancing along the edges. Kalla growled deeply and reached out with her own magick to freeze the disks in mid-air. Immobilized, they folded in upon themselves, resolving into tiny squares small enough to be held in a palm. Artifice weapons then, though she could think of no mage who fought with weapons like these.

The Healer ignored the disks, except to extend her shields to cover them so that her opponent couldn't easily reclaim them. Kalla tried to dart away from another fireball, but was halted by a flame-laced whirlwind that coalesced around her. She grunted as the fireball hit the shields, the energy absorbed. The whirlwind dissipated, absorbed as the fireball had been.

Her opponent became more aggressive, bombarding her with a flurry of fireballs, each burning a fierce blue. They slammed into her all at once and overloaded the absorption shield. It crumpled around her, leaving only the innermost layer of shields to bear the next flurry. These too crumpled, leaving the Healer vulnerable.

Kalla snarled again, her anger building. Ears flat, she used her Alchemy without thinking, to leech the room of all its moisture, rebuilding the air itself to add to it. Gathering it about her, Kalla sent the liquid flood towards the War Mage, encasing him in a watery sphere. She froze it into an icy tomb around him, adding thickening layers to it. He struggled within and cracks began to appear in the ice wall.

The cracks widened and water poured off of the ice sphere faster than Kalla could keep freezing it. She decided to change tactics. As the ice shattered into slushy fragments, she sent her power into the earth and turned the rock beneath the War Mage's feet to viscous mud. He sank quickly and Kalla waited until he was almost completely submerged before solidifying the rock once more. The War Mage began to laugh, amused rather than mocking. The rock turned to sand and he pulled himself free. Holding out his hands in a gesture of peace, he reached up and slipped the hood back.

"Vander...? What the *hells* is going on here? *You* are the new Master War Mage?" Kalla sputtered.

"Yes, Dashkele," Vander replied. He shook his head, freeing the long tail of his mane. Boyish mirth lit his face. "And you passed. You should practice though, to refine those instincts.

"I don't know what is going on. I passed Lord Hauss' test and Lord Sevrus' for Artifice as well though," he continued, stooping to pick up the small metal squares. "With these, no less."

As he touched them, the squares unfurled, turning back into the spiked disks which he spun on his fingers before closing them again and tucking them away. "The Sin' confirmed my position as Master War Mage, now that Cristos is gone. They are hopeful you can bond more of the magi as you have done with Manny, Justina and I."

"I'm not feeling that charitable right now," Kalla grumbled. "I don't appreciate being bundled off like some errant pariah and I am sorry to think you suffered this treatment before and they would force it on you again."

The doors to either side of the room opened to reveal Aelfin and Cara. The magisters recalled their charges. Vander gave Kalla a confident grin as he turned to join Cara. She frowned as she trudged to Aelfin. The Healer's lips thinned, and her ears flattened. She narrowed her eyes at the magister as she walked through the door and the psychic chains settled around her like a pall.

The Sin' of Cryshal

Malik gave the enraged Healer a slight enigmatic smile and set off down the corridor. Helpless, and with Aelfin's presence looming behind her, Kalla was forced to follow. They walked for what seemed an eternity, zigzagging through myriad labyrinthine passageways before reaching a massive set of heavy oaken doors.

Vander was already standing before the doors, guarded by Cara. Justina was nowhere in sight. Malik shared a look with Aelfin and disappeared with a crack of power. After a moment, the great doors creaked open. Cara and Aelfin gently herded them through.

Kalla shivered at the sight that greeted the pair. The chamber was lit by the soft glow of Artifice lamps. At the far end, the entirety of the 'Sin were gathered on a raised dais, looking like a solemn assembly of grim-faced crows in their billowing black judiciary robes. Vander flinched beside her, his ears drooping. Before the dais stood the four House 'Tem.

Cara and Aelfin halted the pair before the Tem' and gently, but firmly, urged them to their knees without speaking. Kalla folded her legs beneath her, but didn't take her fierce gaze from

Justina's, her anger quite palpable. Justina merely gave them a slight smile just as mysterious as Malik's had been, not at all fazed by the Healer's fury.

Justina stepped up to the kneeling magi and placed a hand on their heads. Kalla's ears flattened at the touch.

"*Close your eyes. Do not open them until you are instructed to,*" the 'Tem said. A growl rumbled in her throat. Her displeasure voiced, Kalla let her eyes slide closed.

Justina stood silent before them. There came the gentlest of touches against Kalla's mind, a similar presence as that felt when a new mage was assessed for House placement.

"Fire and fury you have, a strong will to lead. May Balgeras bless you," Justina said. She lifted her hand and moved away.

From his scent Kalla could tell it was Farlyn, the Crannog-marchogi 'Tem of Malkador that took Justina's place. He rested a hand on her head.

"Earth's stability you have, patience and tenacity. May Fen'raal bless you," Farlyn rumbled. He stepped back and was replaced by Shazmina tem'Wyvaldor, a petite Persiali who smelled of saffron and desert sands.

"Ocean ebb and flow you have, mercy and compassion your strengths. May Ottric Roi bless you," she said in her musical voice. Shazmina gave way to the final 'Tem. A whippet thin man originally of the Maracca, Amazu tem'Aerodor smelled of heat-warmed stones and well-worn parchment.

"Wind's sharpness you have, quick of thought and hungry for knowledge. May Aitaxx bless you."

Amazu gave way to another mage. Kalla tensed as she recognised the scent of the Grand Maester himself. He touched her shoulder briefly.

"*Give me your hand,*" Jasper sin'Solidor said. She did so and he gently pulled her up, freeing her magick.

"Rise, Kalla sin'Solidor, Vander sin'Solidor."

Kalla's eyes flew open, shocked. Jasper's eyes glittered in amusement as he offered his congratulations.

She shared a bewildered look with Vander and saw that his robes were now trimmed in the splashes of color marking the 'Sin. Hardly believing it she looked down at her own robes and found them marked thus as well.

"*Congratulations, milady,*" Aleister said. She turned and found him being led in by Aelfin, Kasai the hawk perched on his shoulder. The harrier glided to Vander's shoulder and promptly bite his ear by way of congratulations. Kasai made a grumpy noise and hunched down, glaring protectively as the rest of the 'Sin gathered to welcome the pair to their ranks.

"This was all a *test?*" Kalla sputtered.

"Indeed, Lady Kalla. One we have all been through. Just as unexpectedly too, I might add," Sevrus said with a laugh. "I remember my own initiation. I was stolen away from the Forge one night as I worked late. Ossler had already retired for the evening and I was alone."

"I thought you had all gone mad, tricking us into returning, only to arrest us. Not a fair trick at all Master Sevrus, given what Vander had been through when last he was here," she said in a low voice.

Sevrus glanced over at the War Mage, where he stood talking with Malik and Justina. "No, I agree, but he weathered it well. I'm not sure who was angrier, him or his magister, when they woke.

"He tried to find you, you know. Ossler and Aelfin had a hard time containing Vander without harming him until Malik and I got there. You've won a loyal friend." Sevrus paused a long moment. "And kept us from making a serious mistake. Thank you, Lady Kalla."

Grosso stirred fitfully in his sleep, brought to full wakefulness by the eerie barking cries of the Reavers surrounding his home. The mage paid little mind to them most of the time. His master had sent several more *triths* to join Igasi's, and they had taken up residence in the surrounding forest. The noises they made served as a further deterrent to nosy people poking around in the woods.

Grosso sighed and levered himself up. Sleep was a rare companion these days. He shuffled towards the hearth, flexing the stiff fingers of his right hand as he did so. Irritation creased his features, gone as quickly as it had come, before his thinning face settled into tired lines.

His nights were haunted by nightmares and the Nagali's displeasure. Al'dhumarna had been enraged to learn that Kalla had obtained another tooth from the dragon goddess and no longer need search for the one James now carried. That anger had been further compounded when Grosso had come upon the slavers camp and set the slaves free instead of slaying them along with their captors. Grosso had prevented the *triths* from hunting the slaves down, taking the vicious predators elsewhere to slake their insatiable bloodlust after the camp was destroyed.

The Nagali had set him to making more enchanted equipment, this time to fit the Reavers' needs, not that they needed his help to be deadly. His waking hours were spent carrying out these orders. Slipping a pair of glasses on, he hooked a loupe over one lens and picked up his tools. Hunching over the workbench that covered half of one wall, he began working on the bracer that was his current project.

Alert! Alert!

Heh.... I'm so mean.

This book was never intended to be broken down, so instead I have set it up as a serial, rather than sequels. The entire thing is finished, and the remaining parts should be out in quick succession. Be sure to visit the links provided at the beginning for updates on new works in progress and the status of releases.

I do hope you enjoyed this brief foray into the realm of De Sikkari.

By all means, feel free to contact me:

Twitter: @cala_gobraith
Mail: belsuutcala@gmail.com, include Sikkari in the title or it might be binned as spam.

Lightning Source UK Ltd.
Milton Keynes UK
UKHW022303080321
380016UK00014B/1872/J

9 781034 541080